praise for
quim monzó

"A gifted writer, he draws well on the rich tradition of Spanish surrealism to put a deliberately paranoic sense of menace in the apparently mundane everyday and also to sustain the lyrical, visionary quality of his imagination."
—*New York Times*

"Monzó, in small, masterful strokes, gives his stories a full-bodied existence. . . . Quim Monzó joins contemporary short-story writers such as Etgar Keret and George Saunders with the ability to show the absurd in the real, and how the absurd reveals the real."
—*World Literature Today*

"Quim Monzó is today's best known writer in Catalan. He is also, no exaggeration, one of the world's great short-story writers. . . . We have at last gained the opportunity to read (in English) one of the most original writers of our time."
—*The Independent* (London)

"To read *The Enormity of the Tragedy* is to enter a fictional universe created by an author trapped between aversion to and astonishment at the world in which he has found himself. His almost manic humor is underpinned by a frighteningly bleak vision of daily life."
—*Times Literary Supplement* (London)

other books by
quim monzó in
english translation

The Enormity of the Tragedy

Gasoline

Guadalajara

O'Clock

a thousand morons

quim monzó

translated
from the
catalan by
peter bush

Copyright © 2007 by Joaquim Monzó
Copyright © 2007 by Quaderns Crema, S.A.U., Barcelona, Spain
Translation copyright © 2012 by Peter Bush
Published by arrangement with Quaderns Crema, S.A.U., Barcelona, Spain, 2010
First published in Catalan as *Mil Cretins* by Quaderns Crema, S. A., 1996

First edition, 2012
All rights reserved

Library of Congress Cataloging-in-Publication Data:

Monzó, Quim, 1952–
 [Mil cretins. English]
 A thousand morons / by Quim Monzó ; translated from the Catalan by Peter Bush. — 1st ed.
   p. cm.
 Short stories.
 ISBN-13: 978-1-934824-41-2 (pbk. : alk. paper)
 ISBN-10: 1-934824-41-0 (pbk. : alk. paper)
 1. Monzó, Quim, 1952—Translations into English.
 I. Bush, Peter R., 1946– II. Title.
 PC3942.23.O53M5513 2012
 849'.9354—dc23
                                             2012022677

Translation of this novel was made possible thanks to the support of the Ramon Llull Institut.

LLLL institut
       ramon Llull
Catalan Language and Culture

Printed on acid-free paper in the United States of America.

Text set in FF Scala, a serif typeface designed by Martin Majoor in 1990 for the Vredenburg Music Center in Utrecht, the Netherlands.

Design by N. J. Furl

Open Letter is the University of Rochester's nonprofit, literary translation press:
Lattimore Hall 411, Box 270082, Rochester, NY 14627

www.openletterbooks.org

Contents

1.

Mr. Beneset	5
Love Is Eternal	13
Saturday	22
Two Dreams	32
I'm Looking out of the Window	37
Praise	48
The Coming of Spring	56

2.

Next Month's Blood	79
Thirty Lines	80
A Cut	82
One Night	84
Another Night	87
Beyond the Sore	90
Many Happy Returns	93
Things Aren't What They Used to Be	96
The Fullness of Summer	99
The Boy and the Woman	102
The Fork	105
Shiatsu	108

I

"Hey, guy, let us in."
"You got an invitation?"
They shake their heads.
"No way then."

—Roman Polanski
Rozbijemy zabawe

Mr. Beneset

Mr. Beneset's son walks into the old people's home and greets the girl in reception, a pleasant, sensible young woman who was, in fact, what tipped the balance when he was looking for a carehome for Mr. Beneset, the reason why he opted for this place and not the other one he also liked in the Putxet district. Girl and son pass the time of day. Chat about life in general, about Easter that is just round the corner, about the new asphalt on the road, and about Mr. Beneset's recent state of health. When he feels they have talked enough, the son says, "Well, then . . ." and smiles as if to say, "This conversation is very interesting but I should leave it here and go to his bedroom." Basically tired of having to talk about the same four topics with every friend or relative of every resident, the girl grimaces as if she is thinking, "Hell, I'm also very sorry, but I understand that there are priorities in life, and you are visiting your father." So Mr. Beneset's son walks away from the desk in reception and into the courtyard. He crosses it, crunching the gravel underfoot like a vigorous adolescent, goes into the elevator, up to the third floor, out into the corridor, and down to the bedroom. It is number 309. He knocks with his fingers: tap, tap, tap; gently at first, then more loudly, and finally, as he elicits no response—Mr. Beneset is going so deaf he probably didn't hear him—he turns the door handle and walks in. Mr. Beneset is standing in front of the mirror. He is straightening some lingerie, black and cream lingerie, the sort the French call *culottes* and the English *French knickers*.

"I've always told you to knock before going into a bedroom," says Mr. Beneset.

"I did, father, but you didn't hear me!" replies his son. He shouts, because if he doesn't shout loudly, his father wouldn't hear him now either. He is about to ask him why he stopped using his hearing-aid months ago and what the point of all those visits to the shop on carrer Balmes had been—to make the mould, adjust it, and teach him how to put it on—if the aid is now always in its case and tucked away forgotten in a drawer. But he says nothing because he reckons that if he does say something and (life being life) his father decides to use the hearing aid again, he will be the one with the remit to buy new batteries. And to show him how to put it on yet again, and more than likely they would have to repeat the process of making the mould, because over time that kind of plastic loses its flexibility and, once it has hardened, it can't be adjusted as it could be initially and a new one would have to be made. So he prefers to keep quiet.

"From the time you were a little kid, I've always told you to knock before going into a bedroom. Haven't I always told that?"

The son walks over to his father and kisses him on the cheek. His father returns the kiss, gripping the nape of his neck, so he doesn't move his face away, and kisses him again. The father really loves his son. He is all he has left in the world.

"But it's water off a duck's back to you. People tell you things and you take no notice."

"Father . . ."

"And now you will say that's not true."

Mr. Beneset had had a close shave, and his white mustache was resplendent against his dark skin. He stares hard at his son, "What are you drinking now? Don't drink, right. You've always liked a drink. Your nose is red, and people who drink a lot get red noses. That's why they give drunks a red nose in comics. Stop drinking, I tell you. Just remember what happened to Uncle Toni. Agh, Toni . . . He drank like a fish as well; that's why he ended up an alcoholic. But he had some reason to. His daughter died and his wife left him, poor guy. I've told you that more than once."

Tears well up in Mr. Beneset's eyes, but he acts as if they don't. His son notices he has had a very short haircut. To help him change the subject, he makes a scissors gesture with his fingers and smiles and nods approvingly. Mr. Beneset's face lights up.

"It's better short, isn't it? At my age short hair looks much better. You don't have to worry about combing it. And when you wash it, it dries right away and you don't get pneumonia."

Mr. Beneset takes the bra, that is also black and cream, off the back of the chair. His arms are so thin that when he reaches behind his back to do up his bra, it looks as if they are sure to break. His son goes over to help.

"Let me be, I can do it. I don't need anyone's help. I'm not like all these old guys around here—yet. This place is full of old men. Growing old is terrible. That's why you should look after yourself, while there's still time. Stop drinking. Because I know you drink. You're very fond of drinking. It was so embarrassing that day when your friends had to carry you home, because you were so drunk you passed out. And that's enough talk. It's tiring, you know."

Mr. Beneset moves very slowly over to the sink using his walker. He looks at himself in the mirror and adjusts the bra.

"Bring me the stool."

His son takes him the white plastic stool from under the shower. Mr. Beneset takes the toilet bag from the shelf and sits down. He takes a pink ball from a transparent bag full of variously colored cotton-wool balls. He unscrews the tube of face cream, squeezes it on the cotton and slowly smears his face. Then he applies make-up powder, so his skin isn't shiny. He puts highlights on his lips with a brown pencil and, when he's just about to put on bright red lipstick, someone knocks on the door. It is the girl who is going to make his bed.

"Good day, Mr. Rafael," she greets him.

"Good day, my lovely," Mr. Beneset replies. He addresses his son, "This is Margarita, a really lovely girl. Isn't Margarita lovely? Margarita is Cuban. Cuba is a beautiful country. You've got lots of sugar cane, haven't you, Margarita?" Margarita nods.

When he has finished painting his lips, Mr. Beneset starts on his eyes. He draws one line underneath and another above. He puts brown shadow on his eyelids and orange between eyebrow and eyelid. Then, mascara on his eyelashes. He wheezes. He asks his son to pass him his blouse. It's on a hanger. His son does so. He puts it on.

"Goodbye, Mr. Rafael," says Margarita when she has made his bed. She leaves.

"She is very pretty," says Mr. Beneset. "Make sure the door is shut. I don't want them to hear us. Don't you think she's very pretty? There are lots of pretty girls here, poor things, looking after old crocks. I look at them and feel sorry for them. I think: Poor girls, couldn't they find a better job than looking after old crocks? But, obviously, people go hungry in the countries they come from, and they all *do* come from elsewhere. Margarita is Cuban. From Cuba. But she doesn't eat meat. She's vegetarian. Perhaps you should stop eating meat too? Or perhaps not. Do you look after yourself properly? There's another girl, she's not Cuban, her name is Yuli, she's got nice big boobs; she's lovely. I know it all depends on your pocket around here; if you pay, they soon do for you. And they are so pretty . . . I had to tell them not to give me showers, because my knob went as stiff as a brush. There's one who would say, 'Ooh, Mr. Rafael, what a big one . . . At your age too!' I tell them to let it be, that I'll do that area, because, poor things, it upsets me that they're so young and rubbing an old man's stewed meat. But you bet a lot take advantage of them. And the girls are clean. They wear gloves. Not like the old women who sometimes act as if they've got the wrong bedroom and get in your bed in case you want to do it with them. One wanted me to do it with my mouth. You know what I mean? You get my drift, don't you?"

Mr. Beneset edges towards his bed and sits on it. He rolls on the tights and skirt and puts on the broad, flat-heeled shoes. He takes a paper bag, one with two handles, and puts a bottle of water, a toilet bag, and an old newspaper in it. Mr. Beneset, his walker, and his son go into the passage, take the elevator, and walk through the sitting room to get to the backyard. Two women and a man sitting next to each other on wicker armchairs say hello and gawp vacantly. They find a bench in the yard, Mr. Beneset takes out the newspaper, dusts down the bench, sits down, unscrews the top off the bottle of water and takes a gulp.

"I filled it up before you got here. So I was ready. You come so infrequently, I didn't want to waste a minute . . . I know you've a lot to work on, my boy, I know you have, and I'm not reproaching you for only coming every once in a while."

Mr. Beneset wipes the rouge from the corner of his lips with one of the dozen or so paper handkerchiefs he has spread around his various jacket pockets. Then he combs the quarter-inch high lawn of white hair his barber left him. He always has to keep an eye on her, to make sure she doesn't get carried away with that electric clipper of hers. And you can understand why, Mr. Beneset tells him: a haircut is over in a flash with a clipper and, conversely, it takes much longer with scissors. She gets paid by the number of cuts or by the hour, so his hairdresser is keen on getting the job done as quickly as possible.

"In this place," he goes on, "when somebody dies they say that *he has left*. You know when somebody has died because, suddenly, they're not here anymore. Suddenly, they're not here anymore: not in the garden, not in the dining room, not in the TV room, not anywhere, and they always were, until the day before yesterday. Day one passes: maybe they're ill. But if they've not been around for days and you ask what's wrong, they tell you that they have left. They have left—to go where? They won't tell you. Last week *another guy left*. Sometimes, you hear noises in the corridors at night. Suddenly there are lots of footsteps rushing up and down. They must be removing a corpse, I always think, and reasonably enough, they remove it at midnight so as not to upset the rest of us."

Mr. Beneset looks at his son, and as he's against the light, he can hardly see his face, and he tells him he doubts in the end whether he should have that operation on the cataract on his right eye (they operated on the one on his left eye five years ago, just before the first cancer). But he also says: Why invest all that time and have all those headaches if he knows he's not got much time left and what little he has is far too much anyway? He downs another gulp of water. He notices a film of saliva has accumulated at the corner of his lips and wipes it away with one of the handkerchiefs he is carrying in his pockets, but then he realizes he has smeared his lipstick.

"I've made a real mess, haven't I?"

"No, only a little one. Give me the handkerchief, and I'll fix it."

His son uses the handkerchief to clean up the lipstick he'd smeared on his cheek. He doesn't say that he *never* keeps to his lips and that he always runs over or that the lines he draws by his eyes are crooked.

"Sometimes," he goes on, "I dream they are summoning me from heaven. My mother, my father, all my brothers and sisters: Rafelet, why are you taking so long to come? I am the only one left down here. Ricardo was the first to die. Then, my father, that was . . . How many years ago was it? I don't know how many. Sixty-odd. The most recent was Arcadi, and that was twenty years ago." Mr. Beneset has been a widower for three years. Although his wife is also dead, curiously she never appears in his dreams, begging him to join her. It's only his blood-related family (parents, brothers, and sisters) that shouts down to him. "I have lived twenty years longer than my longest-living brother and I've had enough. I could take one of those pills that put you to sleep, and once you've fallen asleep you don't wake up, because they don't just put you to sleep; when you are asleep they kill you painlessly. The other day I asked the doctor: 'Why don't you give me one and that way it will be over quick?' She scolded me: 'Don't say that—even in jest!' I wasn't kidding. How does she know whether I was kidding or not? I say it for real but nobody believes me. I sometimes look at the window and think how easy it would be to jump out. The difficult bit would be climbing up. If I could climb up, sit there, and pull my legs over the other side, I'd do it straight away. But I'm not strong enough, and I can't ask you to do me that kind of favor."

Some old folk are strolling around the yard and looking at him cheekily. One man, from the bench opposite, is gawping at his legs, his mouth gaping. His son thinks that if he must wear tights, he ought to tell him to take the trouble to shave, but he immediately realizes, that if he took any notice, he'd be the one charged with buying the razors, the wax, or whatever he'd use to get rid of the hair, and so he decides to say nothing. Mr. Beneset looks at his son.

"Come on, let's go back to my room."

"Why do you want to go so soon? We've not been here half an hour."

"I've had enough. Really. I'm tired."

The son helps his father to get up. They walk through the lounge where the two women and the man are still sitting next to each other, staring vacantly. They take the elevator to his floor. Back in his room, Mr. Beneset sits on his bed and looks at his clock.

"It's still some time to lunch. You go; you've got enough going on. And don't rush to come back, I know you've lots of commitments."

They kiss each other, the son turns around, walks away, stops by the door, turns around, waves goodbye to his father, closes the door and uses the handkerchief to remove the lipstick the kiss left on his cheek. While his son is going into the elevator, Mr. Beneset takes out his toilet bag and starts to tidy his hangnails. Then he cuts his nails and files them. Immediately after, he opens the nail varnish and applies a layer. He starts with the small finger of his left hand and finishes with the small finger on his right. When the first layer has dried, he applies the second.

Love Is Eternal

We crash into each other when we walk around the street corner. I am in a rush, clutching my briefcase, my umbrella on my other arm, because, although it isn't raining now, in the evening, when I left home that morning, the sky was gray and a rain that threatened to last till dusk was falling. Carolina was also in a rush, with no umbrella but one of those leather bags that you sling over your shoulder, and two huge, plastic bags embossed with the name and address of a linen shop. We hadn't seen each other for five years. We really crash head on and recognize one another immediately. She says, "Hello," and it's as if she doesn't know which way to look. "Hello," I say, staring straight into her eyes so she doesn't notice that I don't really know where to look either. "What a coincidence," she says, and then she checks herself, as if indicating that she'd like to go beyond the usual clichés: "But you can't really call it a coincidence: we do live in the same city." "How are you?" I ask. "I'm fine," she says, "How long is it since we last saw each other?" "It must be five years," I immediately speculate because, the very moment we bumped into each other, I had thought it must have been five years since our last sighting, as I mentioned before. "Less," she says, "we saw each other that day when you were leaving the cinema." It's true. I hadn't thought of that. One day, months after we'd stopped going out, I was leaving the cinema with Clara and spotted Carolina in the line. She was by herself, and I didn't exchange more than a couple of words with her, precisely because I was with Clara, and later on when I was home I thought of giving her a call, but didn't have her number and, as the hours went by, I started to think it was preferable not to say anything and to let things stay the way they were. In effect, we had seen each other in the entrance to a cinema and that didn't seem excuse enough to call her. Call her to say what exactly? And now I had come across her again, several years later. "I'm fine," I repeat, "I'm fine now but I missed you a lot to begin with." "That means you don't miss me anymore." "Of course I don't. I'd have a screw loose if I was still missing you." "Well I often think about you." "If you think about someone, it doesn't mean you're missing them. I also thought about you that day we saw each other in the cinema line." "But if we hadn't spotted one another you wouldn't have thought of me even then." "I didn't say I never think or have never thought about you."

We look rather absurd, burdened down with our briefcases, bags and an umbrella. "Where did we go wrong?" I say. "Agh, what a thing to say!" she complains, "Please spare me your outbursts, especially so many years after." And, as if she suddenly found the conversation upsetting, she says: "Ah well, I must be going . . ." "I'm going to have a bite to eat, before I go home," I tell her. "So don't you eat supper at home any more?" she asks. "No. I've become more flexible. I sometimes eat in a bar, wherever, so when I get home, it's done with. Why don't you join me?" She makes it obvious that she's wavering for a second.

The café table is white formica. The chairs are white as well. I sit in one, Carolina in another, facing me. The bags, briefcase and umbrella occupy a third. Carolina has ordered a hamburger, with pickled onion and gherkin, and is eating rather slowly. In the old days three hamburgers wouldn't have been enough, and she'd have had them with mounds of chips and salad. She ate a lot, barely put on weight, and was very proud of that knack of hers. Now she eats less, she is even thinner, but she is still the same shape she was five years ago. Plump breasts, a round butt, a gluttonous mouth that never really shuts entirely; not even now, so I can see her top and bottom teeth, and now and then the tip of her tongue that comes out to moisten her lips.

I can't stop my doubled over fingers from dramatizing a character from a children's story, from going—trip trap trip trap—towards her hand on the table, still and expectant, just the right distance away so I can't mount her fingers—trip trap—and caress her. "We shouldn't be doing this," she says. I respond, "I thought if I turned my fingers into a character out of a fairy story you'd accept an approach." She smiles. She was the one who taught me how to turn my hand into a character out of a children's story. When she was a child and was ill—which was often—her father always told her stories. Carolina, Carolina, the beautiful Carolina with whom I had never wanted to live . . . With whom I never had the courage to go and live, she'd say when we argued about it. When the character from a story finally reverts to being a hand that covers and caresses hers, she looks at me tearfully, as if I didn't know how easily tears welled in her eyes. After the hamburger we pop into her place, which is nearby. Only for a moment, to leave the bags from that shop so we can go for a drink without that burden, but once we're upstairs, we don't come down again.

When I leave the next morning, we agree to meet that evening. We have dinner out and go back to her place. We see each other again the day after. Then we don't call each other for three days. She rings me on the fourth. She sounds annoyed: "How come you never call?" "You don't either," I retort. "I thought something must have upset you, or that you'd had enough." "No," I tell her, "I would like to meet up." We meet up, and that night we do nothing but talk about whether we're making a mistake again, whether it's stupid to see one another so often, although a good part of the conversation underlines that we are under no obligation to commit to anything, etcetera. We spend the weekend together at her place, and the next one as well. Sunday night we are in her kitchen, in a scene that augurs the worst routines imaginable: I'm wearing my pajamas and she's in a short-sleeved T-shirt that's three sizes too big for her. One is washing the dishes and the other is rinsing and placing them on the plate rack.

I spend the night tossing and turning in bed. Am I making a big mistake? I wonder if I am about to agree to something I refused years ago. Because, in spite of all the diatribes against making commitments, it seems clear she'll be suggesting one any moment now. Employing what arguments? The need to stabilize the relationship, for example? But it's not a foregone conclusion she will suggest it. Though, if she does, what will I reply? Years have gone by and, after all, the idea I could stop living alone does occasionally buzz around my head. However, in the hypothetical scenario that Carolina does make such a suggestion, if I say yes, it would seem like a terrible concession, because it would be like she'd won the game. But the fact is she has yet to say a word, no doubt because she assumes I wouldn't agree, as happened previously, because I have always believed that pledges are something sacred, so once I make a definitive commitment, it is in effect forever and not something I can renege on after a while. Or perhaps she's just not interested any more? I think if I were now to open the door just a crack, she'd immediately lose any wish to go inside. I toss and turn, and think how she's hardly sleeping on her side of the bed either. In the course of all this tossing and turning we embrace. It's obvious that neither of us is asleep; I switch on the table lamp, Carolina gets up and goes to the bathroom, I hear her peeing, I yawn, watch her walk back and look at me from the foot of the bed. The light of day is starting to come through the cracks in the shutter. After a while, I slap the mattress with my flat hand, inviting her to stretch out by my side. She says no, the alarm clock is about to ring, and that she had better get dressed. I surreptitiously shift my erection to one side. Carolina goes back into the bathroom, emerges half-dressed, takes a blouse from the wardrobe, disappears with her blouse, returns fully dressed, and tells me I can stay in bed longer, if I want. As I feel sleepy, I say I will and smile at her. I hear her closing the door and think how often I'd heard her closing it and recall how horrible it is to live the life of a couple. Here I am again, I say, out of pure lethargy, but then I fall asleep.

I wake up twenty minutes later. I shower, dress, and snoop, inevitably, through the books on her shelf, the little boxes—and doesn't she like her little boxes!—the onyx pipe, and the glass ball with a pagoda inside. You turn it upside down and it fills up with snow. The table is strewn with paper. A letter from the man who manages the flat. A theater program. Folders and more folders. Years ago when I told her she was very untidy, she would reply it wasn't true, the truth was that her idea of order was different than mine. But she stuffed letters, bills, invoices and reminders, everything, into folders, as they arrived, irrespective of their contents. I open a drawer. She was always irritated when I rummaged through her drawers and would appeal to her right to privacy. And what about her personal diary? Did she still write one? Or has she given up that adolescent habit? I open a second drawer. There is an envelope from the gym inside, with their hours.

An unused address book, its pages crammed with shopping receipts. I open a third drawer. A folder full of letters and photos. I appear in the odd photo, from six or seven year ago. I look at the senders on the envelopes. Some men. The boyfriends she's had over the years? I read a few. Why did she never become definitively attached to any of them? There's a map of Hungary, postcards from various countries, a map of the Barcelona metro. I open another drawer. The yellow folder there contains letters from her mother and father, photographs of when she was a kid, at school, on an outing, as a young girl, her primary school reports. The green folder is full of medical papers. A big envelope is on top, from her health insurance company, the same one she had then. There's an X-ray inside and two sheets of paper clipped together. As I read them I break into a cold sweat.

I soon find Carmen's number and agree on a time to meet. She was one of Carolina's best friends years ago, and the only one I feel I can trust. I ask her how much she knows. "Did she tell you?" she asks. "We've been seeing a lot of each other recently," I respond. "You're really back together again? Carolina is lucky to have you with her for the little time she has left." She looks at me, her eyes on the point of tears. I liked Carmen a lot, and when I was going out with Carolina, we would sometimes flirt—we had even kissed on the odd occasion. "But what have her doctors told her?" I ask. "What's she got?"

That evening, when Carolina and I have eaten supper and are strolling between boys jumping on to benches on their skateboards, I suddenly take her hand and say I've been thinking hard and that the truth is that recently we've been meeting on a daily basis and, given that we *are* seeing each other almost daily, I think it makes sense for us to live together. She looks at me incredulously. She is so beautiful. On the pale side, maybe, but she has always been on the pale side. She's the kind of woman that pallor embellishes. She would never go to the beach to get a suntan, even at the height of summer. When she has had her fill of staring at me incredulously, she looks down and says no. Why should we live together? Wasn't I the one who was always saying we shouldn't live together, that the best antidote to boredom was to live separately in our own places and only see each other when we felt like it? "What's changed for you now?" she asks. "Perhaps I've grown up in all these years?" I reply. "Perhaps we grow up without realizing and that's another good reason to live together." "No," says Carolina, but I don't give up the battle and persevere throughout the night. And within a few hours she gives in and we start living together. To keep things simple, for the moment we decide to live at my place, which is much bigger than hers. One trip with a truck is enough to move all her things, and now we wake up side by side every morning.

I try to detect signs of her illness, but everything seems unlikely to a non-believer. Carolina is the same as she has always been since we met up again: laughing, affectionate, with those bright, round eyes you wouldn't say . . . She certainly is pale; but as I said earlier, that's one of her traits. I go out of my way to be pleasant, to become what one might call a loving companion, and the day comes when we decide it would perhaps be well worth getting married. It would make her so happy . . . That's what Carmen tells me—we meet every so often to comment on the state of play. So I suggest the idea, and we get married a week later. At the registrar's, nothing formal: she wears a pearl gray dress and I sport a tie I'd never worn before. Carmen gives me a grateful look and hugs me, while I fantasize about kissing the corner of her lips, and she whispers in my ear that what I'm doing is wonderful, that she will never tell Carolina that I know and, unfortunate as she is, she can be happy to have a man like me. Poor Carolina, I think, and, in order to stop thinking about Carmen's lips while she is talking to me, I try to think about the lips that belong to the person I can now, quite properly, call my wife.

But the days pass by, as do the weeks, and the months. By now we have been living together for a couple. It's not that I'm having a bad time with her, let alone that I want her to die. Absolutely not. But if it hadn't been for the fact she was on the point of death, I would never have gone to live with her, let alone married her. Obviously I can't confront her and ask: "Well then, Carolina, how long have you got left?" Nor can I ask what the doctors she is seeing are saying, because officially I know nothing about these visits, nor that she is sick in any way. On the other hand, wouldn't it be reasonable enough to talk about it now that we are married? But I don't dare ask the question or show an interest in the matter, because the assumption still is that I know nothing, and if I were to say something she might think it over and decide that I had gone to live with her out of pity, and that would destroy her. But with each month that goes by I feel more convinced that she ought to be the one to broach the subject. Why is she hiding it? Why this lack of trust? I start to find the situation annoying. It is obvious my passion for Carolina isn't that strong that I need to live with her, and my thoughts repeatedly revisit the same impasse: I wouldn't be living with her and wouldn't have married her if it weren't for her sickness.

However, not only doesn't she die but when she sees pregnant women or mothers with children in prams she takes my arm and looks tenderly into my eyes. By this stage I imagine other men would be contemplating the prospect of splitting up and divorcing, but I married Carolina with the intention of sticking with her to the bitter end. This was precisely the cause of our arguments years ago: that if I committed myself I would do so forever and wouldn't eventually leave her. Maybe the sickness will get worse and Carolina will die in a few days. If I were to tell her we should split up because I was under the impression she wasn't going to live very long and now, on the contrary, our situation just goes on and on, she would feel so saddened I am sure her defenses would immediately collapse, her condition would deteriorate rapidly, and she would die. And that's not really what I want. I want—or wanted—to keep her company until she dies, not to accelerate her death. I would feel guilty forevermore! Anyway the day comes when we are celebrating our wedding anniversary—we also celebrated the day we went to live together—and Carolina cooks a special supper and, as we're finishing the cake and champagne, she turns very serious, moistens her lips before speaking, and says: "I have something to tell you." I shut my eyes and think: She's going to tell me she's pregnant, that she doesn't know how, but we're expecting a child, and that if we make it to the birth stage, I will soon be a widower with a child round my neck. I'm thinking all this and my head is spinning, but she says nothing of the sort and makes that confession I've been so longing to hear. She tells me the last few years have been very hard, that she hadn't said anything in order not to worry me, but she'd been seriously ill for a number of years, a terrible illness with very little likelihood of survival, but that, in her case, this likelihood had proved possible and she'd finally come through, and is totally sure this is a hundred percent thanks to me, and that if I hadn't crashed into her on that street corner, she probably wouldn't have survived. "I owe my life to you," she says, with a kiss.

Saturday

A lifetime's photos with their corners turned over fit in that shoebox. They're packed in without any kind of order. There are photos from when she was a child mixed up with photos of her as an adult. In sixty years she's never had a minute to organize them into an album. And now that she does finally have the time she can't be bothered, and doesn't see the point in sorting them out at this particular stage in her life. Consequently, black and white and color photos live cheek by jowl. Sepia ones as well: her parents, the cousin who died at the age of three when his head was cracked open by a pot of basil that dropped from a neighbor's window, and herself, as a very young child in lace or a long white skirt or a short skirt and carrying a tennis racquet. She puts the box away in a cupboard, under the accordion folder where she stashes her bills. She puts it underneath because the cardboard lid doesn't shut properly and the folder at least keeps it in place. She always looks at the photos on the dining-room table. She places the box to her left and removes the cardboard lid. She uses both hands to take a bunch of photos and set them out in front of her. There are a lot, and she doesn't exactly stare at them hard. A quick glance reminds her of the smallest detail; she

– Saturday –

has looked at them so often! She now searches for one in particular, where she and her husband, arm in arm, are staring icily at the camera. She doesn't search for long, because, although the pile might seem chaotic to the eyes of a stranger, the passing of the years and the habit of looking at the photos time and again means she always knows in which cluster of the various clusters each photo resides. She immediately finds the one she is looking for, and tears come to her eyes. His hair is greased and glinting and she is wearing a small, tulle hat and carrying a posy of jasmine. Keeping her eyes on the photo, the woman rummages in her apron pocket, takes out some scissors, and, with three determined snips, cuts the photo in such a way that her husband falls to the floor and she is left by herself, missing her left arm where he had looped his right. She had hesitated for a moment, wondering whether she preferred to lose her left arm or to keep it with his clinging on, still there. She immediately places what's left of the photo on top of the heap of the other photos, stoops down, and retrieves her husband off the floor and starts cutting him to shreds, with short, regular snips. Then she looks for other photos where they are together, but there aren't any. When she puts the scissors down, the minute scraps of him make a small pile that her right hand sweeps on to the palm of her left and throws in the trashcan. Then she puts the box of photos back into the cupboard and heaps up his jackets, shirts, pants, and ties. It is all destined for a large plastic bag. She bought a box that was labeled FOR INDUSTRIAL USE at the supermarket. She deposits the bag in the hallway just long enough to tidy her hair and put on her coat.

It is an effort to open the dumpster and an even greater one to hoist the bag inside. When she does manage it, the dumpster top stays open. She couldn't care less. She shakes the dust off her hands and walks to the café on carrer Balmes where she sometimes snacks on a spicy sausage sandwich. After that, she buys croquettes at the delicatessen. She goes home, takes off her coat, puts on her apron, and clears the kitchen table, and when she goes into her small sitting room to watch TV for a while, the photo at the end of the passage catches her eye, the one they had taken in that studio on carrer Manso a week before they got married. It is in a broad, varnished wooden frame, him sporting his greasy, glinting hair, and her wearing a kind of small tulle hat and holding a posy of jasmine. She immediately takes it down, goes into the dining-room, puts the frame on the table, and without bothering to look for the tool-box for the pincers for removing nails, she rips the cardboard off the back and pulls out the photo. With three snaking moves she cuts the photo, in order to separate out the figure of her husband and be left by herself, without her left arm, because if she had kept her left arm, his arm, that was gripping hers, would have stayed in the picture. As a girl, she always used to cut the girlfriends she'd argued with out of her photos, and when it was a group photo—and it was very difficult to cut out one individual without spoiling the entire photo—she would score the faces and bodies of the girlfriends she'd argued with, and score them on the negatives as well, to prevent an unexpected appearance in case she ever made another copy. She put the photo down on one side of the table: all by herself now in her tulle hat and with the posy her one and only arm is carrying. For a moment she contemplates the piece of the photo where he is clinging to a disconnected arm; she doesn't think it strange he is roaming the world attached to an arm that doesn't belong to anyone. She heaps up the scraps of paper, and with one hand sweeps them into her other palm and throws them in the toilet; she immediately pulls the chain, and has to do so repeatedly, because one or two pulls don't suffice to make them disappear. Back in the living room she spots some pants and shirts on the rocking chair in the bedroom. His brown pants, the

- Saturday -

gray ones, two white shirts and one blue, and five ties. They all end up in two plastic bags that she takes down to the dumpster. How long before one of those men comes by with a cart, pokes a stick inside, and finds the shorts and pants? If she were to see one, she would tell him right away. She would really like to see one soon walk down the street in one of his shirts with his initials embroidered on the left hand-side pocket. She goes to the milk bar where she sometimes snacks in the afternoon on an *ensaimada* and decaf latte. She has a bun and a latte, buys a bottle of milk, and goes home. She switches on the TV. She keeps changing channels. There's nothing interesting on. She switches it off, picks up a novel she's been halfway through for a week, looks for her bookmark, and starts reading. Five minutes later she realizes, as has happened every time she has tried over the last few days, that she isn't registering a word. She puts the novel down on a coffee table, and then spots the book he was reading—it's upside down in a corner. She opens it at his page: "As we have already seen, a calculation of the frequency with which the letters appear in the cryptogram provides invaluable clues for whoever wants to find the solution." She rips the page out, screws it into a ball, and throws it on the floor. She reads the beginning of the next page—a sentence only—rips out the page, screws it into a ball, and throws it on the floor. She rips the book down the middle, along the spine and, thanks to the American-style glue, tears off the pages one by one. She finishes the job off in the kitchen, above the trashcan, so the pages fall inside. Then she puts the lid on the can, and when she is about to turn around, she notices rolled-up pants' legs in the heap of foul dirty clothes that has been piling up in a corner for days. She goes over, rummages around, and finds two more pairs of pants and five shirts. As she collects them, she sticks them in the trashcan, and as it soon fills up, she extracts the full bag, takes out an empty one, and sticks the shirts in that she couldn't fit in the full one. When she's done, she puts the bags in the hall, goes to the bathroom, and tidies her hair in front of the mirror.

She is carrying a bag in each hand. Before reaching the dumpster she sees a man, with a cart, who is raking inside with a broom. The man is wearing a mask. When did he last take a shower? She hands him the bags. "Here are some shirts and pants."

Rather than just taking it, the man snatches it suspiciously. He deposits the bags in the cart, opens one, and unfolds the shirt, looking thrilled. My God! thinks the woman, next to those filthy paws even the shirts that needed washing seem clean. The man slips one over the shirt he is already wearing. The woman turns around and walks up Balmes, peering into the shop windows. Then she turns left and goes home. She takes off her coat and puts on her apron. What will she do now? Tidy. Tidying up all day and it's never done. For the moment, she thinks, she has emptied the bedroom wardrobe. As she is not altogether sure, she takes another look. Right: not a handkerchief in sight. Nothing on the night table either. Perhaps there are some shoes in the hall cupboard? Several pairs—and a large parcel. When she tears the paper round the parcel, she finds two boxes containing two unused pullovers. She shuts the boxes. She takes off her apron, puts on her coat. The elevator takes its time, because first it goes down without stopping at her floor and then comes back up to a lower floor and then goes down and up again. Finally it arrives.

She goes to the dumpster, opens it, and, as best she can, because it is so full, stuffs in the boxes of pullovers. A passerby chides her for not putting the cardboard in the blue dumpster. The woman doesn't give him a glance. When she has finished, she shakes the dust off her hands, goes to the café on Balmes and drinks a tiny cup of black coffee and a glass of *anís*. Then she goes to the supermarket, buys two more boxes of trash bags, walks home, takes off her coat, slips on her

- Saturday -

apron and sits in front of the TV. She repeatedly changes channels, and then, when she sees an advertisement with a son and daughter giving their parents a wedding anniversary cake, she remembers that, for their thirty-fifth anniversary, their older son gave them a present of two T-shirts imprinted with the photo of the two of them; it was taken in that photographer's studio on carrer Manso, him with his hair glinting and greasy and her in a small tulle hat and with a posy of jasmine in one hand. Where can those T-shirts have gotten to? She looks in the wardrobe, in the T-shirt drawer, but they aren't there. She finds them mixed up with his, well, that is to say, three of his vintage undershirts she drops on the floor for a moment, because what she is looking for now are the photos where they are arm in arm. She searches the other drawers. The ones for underwear, stockings, and socks; she takes a pair and adds them to the two T-shirts on the floor. She searches the upper shelves, among the blankets and eiderdowns, among the jerseys and the box where she keeps wristwatches. She takes two from this box and adds them to the heap of socks and T-shirts.

She finds the T-shirts in the kitchen, in the rag-drawer. She didn't remember deciding to turn them into rags. They are cut in two. There's nothing on the back: it's all white. The photo is on the front. His hair, glinting from all that grease, is a dark patch, and her posy of flowers, a white, unrecognizable blob. She takes the scissors from the front pocket of her apron and carefully cuts out his figure from both T-shirts, and snips it into shreds above the trashcan so the bits don't fall on the floor. When there's nothing left, she returns the other bits of T-shirt to the rag-drawer, gathers up the T-shirts, watches, and socks she left in the bedroom, stuffs them in the bag, takes off her apron and puts on her coat, walks to the dumpster, then thinks about stopping in the café, decides not to, and goes straight home, wondering whether she is being thorough enough.

She decides she isn't. She puts her apron on over her coat and again looks in the box of photos for the piece of the photo where she doesn't have her left arm. She soon finds it. It is one of the first in the pile. She gives it one last glance, and then rips it into shreds that she gathers up in one hand and throws into the bag of trash. The piece of T-shirt that she had put away in the duster drawer also ends up there, in tiny bits. As does the broad, varnished wooden photo frame that was at the end of the hall. She immediately goes to the wardrobe and takes out the drawers where he always kept his socks and T-shirts. She drags them to the elevator one by one, puts them inside, except for the one keeping the elevator door open, goes back, takes off her apron, tidies her hair, takes the bag of trash, and gets into the elevator. A neighbor shouts: "Elevator! What's up?" She stacks the drawers on the ground floor next to the entrance and starts to make trips to the dumpster. On her first she carries a drawer in one hand and the bag of trash in the other. She drags a drawer along on each of her subsequent trips. When she finishes, she rests for a while in the café on Balmes and has milk chocolate with a sugar bun while she watches the cars drive by, hooting their horns. Then she goes home, takes off her coat, puts on her apron, drinks a glass of water and gathers up the hangers where he'd hung his jackets, shirts, and pants and sticks them in a big bag. She takes the toolbox from the sideboard and puts it on the kitchen top. She uses a screwdriver to remove the doors from the wardrobe. She puts on her coat and drags the doors as far as the elevator. It takes her two trips to get them downstairs. She returns home, carries the chairs to the elevator and takes them down in four journeys. She also makes one trip per armchair. She goes straight back home, takes off her coat, puts on her apron, turns the table over and unscrews the legs. As school is letting out, she decides not to make any more trips, because from now on, for a few hours at least, there will be a constant stream of parents and kids.

- Saturday -

She piles everything up in the hallway and waits for evening, so she can take off her apron, tidy her hair, put on lipstick and take it all out to the street.

She orders a plate in the café on Balmes: fried egg, fries, and a tomato sliced down the middle. She goes home, takes off her coat, puts on her apron, strips off the counterpane, bed linen top and bottom, pillows, and pillowslips. As well as what's in the wardrobe. She sticks part in the bag where she'd put the hangers; the others in two more bags. She takes off her apron and puts on her coat. She puts all three bags in the elevator and pushes the foam mattress until she gets it in as well. She finds an old man waiting on the ground floor by the elevator who gives her and her cargo a look of surprise and says, "Good night." She replies with a "Good night," pulls out the mattress and leans it against the wall. "Leave that, leave that, I'll help you," the man tells her. "No, really, there's no need," she responds as she takes the bags out of the elevator and puts them next to the mattress. She has to make three trips to the dumpster, one with the mattress, the second with two bags and the third with just one. She also takes the television and the rocking chair down. When she is back home, she takes off her coat, puts on her apron and dismantles the window that looks over the square. She puts it in the hall. She extracts a hammer and chisel from the toolbox in the kitchen and spends some time attempting to pry the window-frame from the wall. She starts levering with the chisel in the small crack she has managed to make after a few minutes. She gradually chisels pieces out, until the absence of one of the four sides enables her to lever the other three out more easily. When—after putting on her coat—she takes it all to the dumpster, it is nighttime and there are few people in the street. She goes to the café on Balmes, but they have already pulled down the metal shutters and switched off the lights. They are hard at it inside: putting chairs on tables, sweeping and washing up. She goes home, brews coffee, shuts off the water supply and, with the wrench, unscrews the screws that hold down the toilet bowl. Then she detaches it from the pipes and finally, after a few kicks, the bowl gives way and falls on to the floor. She drags it to the hallway. She also unscrews the taps from the washbasin, and the basin falls on the floor and cracks. The shower tray also cracks, because she has to wrench it out with the chisel. She drags it to the landing, takes off her apron, puts on her coat and gradually stuffs everything in the elevator, and from there—in several trips—takes it to near the dumpster, because the dumpster has been full for hours, and all around it is chock-a-block too. Then she goes home, takes off her coat, puts on her apron and starts levering out the tiles. First, from the bathroom walls. Then, from the kitchen walls, and every single floor tile. Many tiles crack, because she often misses the chisel and the hammer smashes against the tiles. Very few emerge intact. Shortly the city police come and tell her a neighbor has complained about the noise. She apologizes, and when the police have gone, she heaps the tiles in the hallway: then she takes off her apron, puts on her coat, loads the tiles into her shopping trolley—because the bags couldn't take the weight—and has to make trips throughout the night. Sometimes she thinks: Maybe this isn't the time to be making so much noise. But she doesn't want to wait till morning; she wants everything to be sorted by sunrise. But it is too much work for her to finish before daybreak. When there isn't a single tile left in the flat, she wrenches the front door from its hinges. She takes off her apron, puts on her coat and, when she is dragging the door down to the dumpster, the black of the sky is beginning to be streaked with dark blue. She goes home, takes off her coat, puts on her apron and starts scraping the paint from the dining room with a scraper. Then, the bedroom walls. Then, what used to be the kids' bedroom. Then, the hallway. Then, the passage. When the plaster on all the walls is

- Saturday -

exposed, she sweeps up the paint scrapings, sticks it in sixteen bags, and—after combing out the dust that had got into her hair, taking off her apron and putting on her coat—she takes the sixteen bags down to near the container. She knocks the dust off her hands, goes to the café on Balmes and, as it is now open again, has a coffee, three donuts and a glass of *anís*. She goes home, takes off her coat, puts on her apron, sits in one corner, and stares at the bare walls, ceiling and floor. It is daytime now and the light gradually spreads through the rooms. It is Saturday and that is why it is silent everywhere. On the stairs, in the other flats, and out on the street. Almost everybody is still asleep. She puts her hands into her apron pocket and plays with the scissors. She takes them out and jabs the sharpest point at the skin on the thumb of her left hand, near the nail, and once she has finally made an incision, she puts the scissors down and with her right hand gradually starts to pull the skin away. Now and then she stops and wipes the blood on her apron.

Two Dreams

The Bachelor Pad

I think it would be right to say I met Beristain when we were on the editorial board of one of those magazines which were once called counter-cultural, and after that we bumped into each other at other magazines, in bars and, later, on the radio. We became close friends, supported one another's alibis and bar antics and, as we both had a fair number of casual liaisons and visits to rooming houses were costing us a fortune, we decided to rent a room on the carrer Cubí, right across from two of the city's most fashionable late-night bars, so we could be chatting up a girl, coming on hard, and say: "If you want, you can get it up in a flash." The girl would always smile incredulously: "Oh, really? The bathroom in this bar is too small." "I don't mean in the bathroom here. I've got a studio flat across the street." The fact that you had a studio across the street from the city's most fashionable late night bars intrigued them. We split the flat in two, so we both had two small rooms: one inside and the other looking over the street. We shared the hall, kitchen and bathroom. We knocked the walls down with a mallet.

When Beristain separated from his wife, he moved in. I would go in and out, but he was always around, discreetly shut up in his rooms, with some girl or reading. This division of space was only disrupted when we both ended up in bed with two girls, and then we'd use one bed or the other, depending on how it was going. We sometimes gave the keys to a friend, so I might find someone else in Beristain's rooms, or he would find someone in mine.

When I was the one who separated, I would still go there and kept up the appearance of the unattainable that the possibility of taking girls home—real home—disrupted. But I soon tired of maintaining a bachelor pad when I was living by myself, and I gradually stopped going. Several months, even a year or so, passed like that until I told Beristain that I would never go back. We decided that from then on we'd no longer split the rent and that he would pay it all, although we kept the lease in my name to avoid an increase in the rent. This situation lasted for several years, until the building was bought by one of these companies that buy real estate, throw out the tenants, refurbish the flats and re-sell them at incredibly high prices. The manager of the block called us in one day and gave us money to vacate the flat, and Beristain went to live in Sant Cugat, in a flat above the one where his mother lived.

But in the dream I had immediately after Beristain died of cancer none of this had happened. Beristain had certainly died a few months earlier, but I hadn't separated and the flat was still serving as a bachelor pad, although I never went because I didn't have the time. Until one night, the night I had this dream, I did go. I take a girl with me, who starts kissing me on the stairs. But, when I open the door with my key, I find a flat full of people. People in both halves of the flat, Beristain's and mine, in all four rooms, and in many others that suddenly appear, because the pad has grown much bigger, with lots of spaces that the real pad never had. There are very high walls, and pointed arches. But even though there is more space, there isn't room for everyone. There are so many people—dozens, perhaps a hundred men and women fucking on the beds, piling in as best they can—that there's no empty space. There are so many people they don't fit in the rooms, and they have to make a line outside the doors, waiting their turn to go in. While they wait, they kiss, caress, fondle . . . When they see me come in, they give me odd looks, as if they are wondering, "Who is this guy?" or, "What's he up to now?" I wonder: "What are these people doing here, where do they come from, what are they doing in my flat?"

I soon discover what has happened: Beristain gave his key to someone, before he fell ill. This someone had a copy made. And someone else made a copy of this friend's key and he in turn gave it to someone else who made another copy. When Beristain died, the pace accelerated and, one after another, everybody kept giving the key to someone else to make copies, so that by now hundreds of people in the city have a copy of the key to the flat and use it when they want.

I am annoyed they are so brazen, furious at them (because they keep passing on copies of the key to a flat that isn't theirs) and at Beristain, because he gave out the key with characteristic gusto and lack of foresight. I decide to change the lock in the morning, and kick them all out. I separate the ones who are fucking so unceremoniously—and when cocks and cunts separate out, they slurp and drip—and I tell them to clear off. Like true inhabitants of dreams, they offer no resistance and walk out, putting on half their clothes as they go downstairs, disappointed they can't fuck where they thought they could, but not particularly stressed or upset. And while they are leaving I think what they have done is an abuse of trust, but then all of a sudden I wonder if I've not gone too far by throwing them out like that and whether I ought not to have been more understanding and waited for them to finish what they were doing. Because, if they all have keys and run around the flat as if it were theirs, I am also partly to blame for abandoning it for so long, for not going there more often, for not enjoying life with the same gusto and frivolity that Beristain displayed.

Paternity

The first time I heard Brugat's voice in person was on the intercom at the radio station where he then worked, on the Via Augusta, and it was to tell us—Lolita and me—that before going up to the studio we should go to the only bar that was open nearby, the Maria Castaña, and buy a few beers. We went to the Maria Castaña, I bought the beers and I went up the stairs to the radio station, loaded down. We chatted, he interviewed me, and afterwards we went to a dreadful pizzeria that was also nearby.

Five years later we worked together at a new radio station. Brugat, Beristain and I on the same program. Brugat was the kind of person who survived on the minimum; he was the individual with the least interest in having children I had ever known, and I have known lots. When I told him that Lolita and I had decided to have a child, he responded: "So, it's for real then?" Several years later, we met in the street when I was coming back from picking our kid up from his school; we went into a bar for a drink, and he stared at my son like he was an alien, or like the poet Pere Gimferrer did the day we shared a taxi from a TV studio on the outskirts of the city, where we had recorded an advertisement to promote reading—Gimferrer had gawped at our kid, pointed his finger at him, and said to me, as if seeking confirmation: "That is a child."

Then it was the cancer. Brugat got cancer, put his trust in a man who gave him his blessing from afar—from Saragossa—and died. In the dream I had just after he was buried, Brugat is dead and has two lovely children: a two-year-old boy and a five or six-month old baby girl, who, despite being so young, was chatting away very wittily and showing great wisdom. Her huge eyes miss nothing. She is very cute and is drooling a lot.

Brugat, as ever, is smiling and wearing his worn and smelly black fur hat. He seems very happy, blissfully so, the man who never showed the slightest interest in having children. Who knows why, but finally, he has had some. He is a late father, right on the precipice. He waited so long to have children, got so near the precipice, that they were born when he was already dead—the two-year old as much as the five or six month-old baby girl. However, even so, he looks after them and plays with them, and the kids are incredibly content with their father—as if I were the only person in the world who knew that he is dead—and a beaming, bright-eyed Brugat shows them off to me, immensely proud of his offspring.

I'm Looking out of the Window

I'm looking out of the window, not because I don't have anything else to do, because I always have a pile of things to do—I'd prefer a lot less—but because, if the truth be told, I don't feel like doing any of them. I feel like looking out of the window. I'm looking out of the window and contemplating the building opposite. Nothing special. Two balconies lit up, the curtains open, everything else in darkness. Through one balcony you can see an empty table in a dining room. Through the other, a room, a door, and a stretch of bare wall. There must be furniture too, probably a bed, because a shirt and pants are on a hanger behind the door. Nothing stirs. I've been looking out for some time and feel thirsty and should go and drink a glass of water, but if I get up, I'd stop looking out of the window and if I do that, I bet I would get sidetracked into doing whatever and wouldn't take another look. It isn't as if I've derived great pleasure from this activity in all the minutes I've spent looking out, because there are only those two balconies lit up. I lie down. Now I'm paying proper attention, there is a terrace a lot further up, with a woman ironing on a board and a child in a playpen who has just bounced his rattle on the ground. I hadn't noticed this balcony before because it is so high up—to see it I have to stoop forwards and stare up and, until now, I had had a decidedly cavalier attitude, staring at the other two balconies beneath mine that I can see without any need to stoop.

What about the street? I'd have to be closer to the window to see the street. Perhaps it's high time I did so, to broaden my field of vision, and because my back is hurting from keeping still for so long. So I move closer. I could only see the building opposite from where I was before. I can now see the street as well. A car drives by. Before it comes into view you hear a noise, it's approaching, it reaches its loudest when it passes under the window and disappears when it turns the corner into the avenue. Now a motorcycle passes by, making a din, and a youth, wearing a black helmet, that brings to mind a huge ant. You can't see any ants from the window, giant or otherwise. Or in the flat or on the street. It's been a long time since I saw an ant. When I was a kid, I used to see a lot, even in the street. There were anthills that we kids would raid on evenings when we were bored with playing soccer. Are there no longer ants in Barcelona? Have they exterminated them all? Have they gone into hiding? Have they migrated to the suburbs? That can't be right, because they sell ant-killer in the supermarket, and if there were no ants, nobody would buy it and they wouldn't stock it. There were plenty in the flat where I lived from the age of twenty-nine to forty-two. They would come in via the gallery and head for the kitchen and I'd scatter a sort of white powder along their route that I had bought at the grocer. A draughtsman lived two floors above the grocer. One night I saw him fucking on his drawing-table. The girl was sitting on the table, legs apart, and he was in front, standing up, moving in and out of her. I can't see any draughtsman or drawing table from the flat where I live now. I can see a dog, with its kennel on a balcony. Sometimes it spends the whole day alone on that balcony, howling. I've never had a dog, I don't really like dogs, but I'm sorry for the dog because it spends the whole day alone. You can't see it now. Perhaps it has gone inside its kennel.

I look through the window and see a woman crossing the road. There are two cars that have stopped, their snouts a yard from the pedestrian crossing. They don't usually stop so far away. Car snouts usually invade pedestrian crossings with the arrogance of a conquistador. The woman crossing the road is dragging a shopping trolley with one hand and, as it couldn't take everything, she is carrying a supermarket bag in the other. The telephone rings. Luckily it's on the table, within arm's reach, and I can unhook it and still look out of the window. It's Mònica. She asks me what I'm doing. I tell her I am looking out of the window. No, she says, I'm not asking you what you are doing right now, but what you are doing in a more general sense. I tell her that it is in the more general sense that I am looking out of the window. I've been doing so for quite some time. In fact—I lift my wrist up, so my watch is in front of the window, so I can consult it with one eye and still look out of the window with the other—I have been looking out for a good three and half hours. It's now almost twelve, and I must have started at around half past eight. Mònica asks me what I can see out of my window that makes it so worthwhile. I can see the street, the building opposite, and the trees, and, as it's winter, I can see a section of the avenue. She says: If you lived actually on the avenue, you would see much more when you looked through your window. This is an avenue in the local neighborhood, a quiet avenue without masses of people, or clowns with made-up faces creating a spectacle. What would I see there that I don't now? I'd see many more dogs, that's for sure. People like to walk their dogs there, for a piss and a shit, because there are areas of grass and, even though the sign forbids walking dogs on the grass, everybody takes their dog to piss and shit there. And given that they scratch the ground with their hind legs after they have pissed and shat, there's no grass left in a number of places. The old woman who feeds the pigeons is even more responsible for the disappearing grass. She is a slightly built, peroxide blonde, and always wears a red coat. *She* doesn't tread on the grass, but scatters the soft bread all over, so that the pigeons throng there in their hundreds to peck at the bread and, as they peck at the bread, they also peck at the turf: the lawns are done for, more brown earth than green grass. This is what I can't see when I look out of the window, and what I would see if I lived on the avenue. I would also see the band that, every other Sunday, plays *sardanas* at midday. I can't see it from my widow, but I can hear the music if I open the window. If I lived on the avenue, when I looked out of the window I would see the people dancing, but I couldn't care less about that, because I have no interest at all in seeing them dance. Conversely, I don't find the music unpleasant. Mònica says: I don't know if you realize this, but you talk more about what you can't see than what you really can see. I reply: That's because you've encouraged me to talk about what I can't see, by saying that if I lived on the avenue I'd see more when I looked out of the window. Besides the fact that the activity of looking out of the window also involves being aware of everything you can't see through the window and everything you're not doing because you are hundred percent focused on looking out. If I weren't here, I'd be doing a bunch of other things. I would be in the kitchen, I would be reading, eating, changing the sheets, putting the washing machine on, and watching TV. As I am looking through the window, I can't do any of that. I can talk to you, for sure, because I can still look out of the window when I'm on the phone. I could listen to music as well, or the radio, and perhaps I will in a while, if I manage to get to the sound system and switch it on and tune into the radio station or put the CD in without taking my eyes, not off the window, but off the things I can see through the window. Mònica asks: Do you often look out of the window? From time to time; but never as intensely as this, with this overwhelming awareness that one is really *looking out of the window*, and channeling all one's attention into this activity. There are lots of people who look out of the window, a quick glance, being nosy, or to pass the time. I have often looked out in that way. But this time it is different. This time it is about concentrating on *looking out of the window*, not to see this or that or to spy on the neighbors. In fact, it would be all the same if I couldn't see anything. If there were a thick fog outside, I would still continue to look out with the same energy and would derive the same high level of pleasure—it's not about what I do or don't see through the window, but the act of looking out in itself. Well, says Mònica, as you are so busy looking out of the window, I'll call you some other time. Don't hang up, I retort; the fact I'm focused on looking out of the window doesn't mean I'm not listening; I'm being really attentive to you. I wouldn't pay you more attention if I weren't looking out of the window. Right now I could be talking to you about this and that, and, if I hadn't told you I'm looking out of the window, you wouldn't have known. Indeed, I have to thank you—it was only when you started talking to me that I became wholly conscious of the extraordinary import of this act of looking out of the window. I doubt that anyone in the world has ever looked out of the window with the same devastating conviction that I am now: the conviction that I have transformed a banal act into a futile obsession to which I will have devoted a few hours and, then, forgotten forever; or at least I hope so. When you asked me what I was doing, I told you, "I'm looking out of the window," as I might have said I was behind my table, or sitting on my swivel chair. Because I am behind my table and sitting on my swivel chair, every single moment I am looking out of the window. Nonetheless, from the moment I opted to tell you that I was looking out of the window the situation has turned into something quite singular. It is very likely that on another day—or maybe even today—I will take another look through the window, but possibly never, ever, will I do so with such fervor and dedication. At least, with that glee in discovering an unexpected possibility in this life where everything is so familiar. Oh, well, says Mònica, I'll call you later, and she hangs up.

Hang up, if you want, I don't care, because the only thing I'm interested in now is looking out of the window and shutting myself off from the rest of the universe. All this time I've been looking out of the window, I've not thought about work, the family, or any of the problems that keep me awake at night. I've not thought, say, about the life I normally lead, or about how I spend my day pondering how things should be rather than savoring them as they come along. I do all I can to put reality in the right frame and to foresee everything so that, if I can avoid any surprises, tomorrow will be all the more tolerable. But foreseeing everything creates such boundless disquiet that things pass me by like a breath of air and I enjoy nothing. I only enjoy a kiss when it is over and done with; then I remember it with pleasure. I don't enjoy it at the time because, beyond the tenderness, I see the darkness, the horrific possibilities lurking behind all that is pleasant. A kiss from my son, for example. I don't enjoy the softness of his cheeks or the happiness in his eyes, because I have to be careful nothing happens to him and warn him of all the dangers in life; not to climb over the balcony rail, not to get into a stranger's car and to chew each mouthful of sandwich twenty times. All this blinds me so much that I only feel delight in the kiss when, half an hour later, my son is asleep in bed and I sit down and relax on a chair in the kitchen and light a cigarette. I lose out on my son's kiss, on friendship, love, laughter, relaxing at night and the pleasure of idleness. And evidently I regret missing out on today so that, when tomorrow comes, a tomorrow I have prepared down to the minutest detail so nothing goes awry, I long for everything I didn't savor at the time, but it would be worse not to foresee things and who knows what might happen . . . what indeed? There is always a threat I haven't anticipated. And, when I wake up tomorrow, yesterday's tomorrow is today's day. Consequently, I miss out on everything good it has to offer, because I spend the whole day anticipating to the nth degree the dangers that the threatening, new tomorrow holds in store. All this time I have been looking out of the window I've not thought about any of this, and the mere fact I am now weighing up all these things derails me and means that—although I continue to stare at what I can see through the window—I'm not doing so with the same intensity as a while ago, when I looked out of the window, and only that, and only thought about what I could see. Consequently, I try to eliminate from my brain everything that isn't what I can see and, to fight off temptation, I remind myself afresh that I am looking out of the window, that this is my goal, and that I mustn't be distracted, at least for a good while. I am looking out of the window. I am looking out of the window. What can I see now? A messenger parking his motorbike on the pavement and taking a fat, white envelope from the metal box he's carrying on the pillion. He presses one of the door bells. After a while I can see him moving his lips by the intercom, and can hear the dreadful juddering of the door as it opens; the messenger pushes it and walks in. A boy walks past on the right carrying a rucksack that is bigger than he is. Suddenly a flock of squawking parakeets appears. A hundred, if not more. They fly leftwards, as far as the esplanade the street broadens into when it meets the avenue; suddenly, the moment their squawks are beginning to fade, the sound resurges because the whole flock returns, heading towards the avenue, where the squawks definitively disperse and disappear into the distance. The messenger now exits from the stairs where he had gone in, puts his receipt book in the pocket of his dark blue jacket and places a brown envelope on the metal box at the back of his bike. My concentration starts to go again. If I don't force myself to stare obsessively at things, my mind drifts off elsewhere. Maybe it is time I stopped looking out of the window? I've been at it too long. The flock of parakeets flies back, once again from the street to the avenue. The messenger revs his bike up. The man from the printer's on the ground-floor of number 31 walks out into the street, crosses to the bar next to my house that I can't see even if I hang my head out of the window. Maybe three and a half hours is the most one can look out of the window with the intensity and concentration I have just devoted to the activity. The messenger pushes his bike from the sidewalk on to the road, jumps the red light and disappears in the direction of the avenue. But maybe I could last until five or six o'clock. Years ago, when there were hardly any distractions, people would spend hours looking out of the window. In villages you still, sometimes, see shadows watching the street from behind windows. Woman at your window . . . How did that proverb go? In whose room I can only make out the door and a stretch of bare wall, a door that now opens. A gentleman walks in wearing an old-fashioned singlet and goes into the part of the room I can't see. The flock of shrieking parakeets flies back. A butane gas truck parks on the curb, and a man gets out of the cabin and starts hitting a rod against the bottles so the noise advertises his merchandise. He is soon walking up and down with three bottles in his cart. I could call Mònica and tell her that if I'm still looking out of the window, I'm not doing so as intensely as when she phoned me, with that overwhelming awareness with which, for the first and perhaps only time in my life, I had been really *looking out of the window*, focusing fully on the act, and maybe at any moment I'll stop doing so. The man who'd left there a short time ago goes back into the printer's at number 31. The flock of squawking parakeets flies back—from left to right. And, the man in the old-fashioned singlet re-appears in the room of which I can see only the door and a stretch of bare wall; after a while he opens the windows, comes out on to the balcony, leans over the balcony with all the time in the world, and looks idly down at the street.

Of course I could stop—now, right now—looking out of the window. In fact, the more the minutes pass the more this activity bores me. I could let it be, get up, go to the bathroom, look myself in the face and shave. I have a two-day-old beard. If I don't know what to do, I could shave. I could turn on the hot-water tap, wait for the water to become tepid, wash my face, shake the shaving soap, squeeze some on my hand, spread it over my face, leave it for a minute or two (or three, or even more) so the foam impregnates my skin and the blade doesn't draw blood. Then I could shave slowly, rinse my face with cold water, and dry myself on a towel and, when I lean close to the mirror to see if any area of my face wasn't properly shaved, I would see a hair on my nose. I can feel it now, because I'm holding it between the index and thumb of my right hand. If I've stopped looking out of the window and have decided go and shave, I'd first look for the long, narrow, sharp-pointed scissors, a barber's scissors. I would cut off that long hair and take the opportunity to check the sides of my nose, in case any others were lurking there. I have a number on my left ear, but none on my right. When I've finished with all the nose hair, I would look at myself in the mirror: my puffy face and bleary eyes. Then, before moving on to the hairs on my right ear—that also deserve some attention, though there are less—I would carefully place the scissors on the lobe of this same left ear and all at once close them quickly in order to get a clean cut. Half the ear would sail through the air and land on the kitchen counter. I would observe it warily. Bleeding gristle. I'd wrap it in a towel. Blood would gush from the ear, though maybe less than what I'm now imagining, as I look out of the window. I'd wash with cold water and take gauze from the jar and wrap it around my ear. I'd put on my shirt, jacket, a sea-blue woolly hat and pull it right down. I would take the towel with the piece of ear, go out and lift my right hand to stop a taxi. "To the Clinical Hospital, quick!" I'd tell the driver. "Which entrance?" he'd ask, aware it was serious. "Emergencies!" Maybe it's not the best time of day? Let's suppose there is a lot of traffic: people going home from the office, people going shopping, children leaving school, parents waiting for them, balancing their backsides on the safety bars they always put in front of schools. Before we reach the hospital, I'd feel the blood soaking the entire hat. "Watch out! Don't stain the seat!" the taxi driver would say. He would turn up on to the ramp to emergencies, right behind an ambulance, its siren blaring. The ambulance would park further inside, at the back, in front of some transparent, flexi-plastic doors, the sort that seem so functional, so *hospital*-like. I'd pay for the taxi, get out, walk to the counter where they admit you, take my hat off, show them my sliced, bloody ear, and also the towel with the piece of ear inside. They would immediately put me on a trolley-bed, and I'd shut my eyes and, feeling rather queasy, would fall asleep with the jolts from the wheels. Then the whole process would start. The questions—how did you do it?—the process of recovery . . . I expect I'd spend a few days in the hospital. This would mean that, for that period of time, however long it might be, I'd not be able to try to solve tomorrow's problems: those at work, those with the family, all the many problems that kept me awake at nights. Maybe I'd be even more stressed out in the hospital by my inability to find solutions to them. So I would soon be wanting them to discharge me: to be able to go home and devote my time to anticipating everything, to warning my son of all the dangers out there: not to climb over the balcony rail, not to get into any stranger's car, to chew each mouthful of sandwich twenty times, and only when all potential perils were under control, would I sit down and look out of the window again, trying—as I'm doing now—trying not to focus on the detail of things, trying to see their volume but not the surface or colors, and later trying to see only the colors, and not the volume or the surface. But it is really very difficult. On the corner, the butane gas truck revs its engine and maneuvers before driving off. The flock of squawking parakeets flies back over—from right to left, yet again.

Praise

One December afternoon, the writer Daniel Broto goes into a bookshop. It isn't one of the bookshops he usually visits in the city center. This one is in a hilly, residential district he wasn't at all familiar with until a cousin of his from Montpeller went to live there a few years ago. Lunch at his cousin's had finished at three and they'd said their goodbyes at a quarter to four, and as Broto didn't have any university classes that day or anything special to do, he decided to walk back downhill. He soon came across the bookshop. He was surprised it wasn't small and pokey, but had numerous, well-stocked shelves; he thought decent bookshops only existed in the city center. He browses among the piles of books stacked on the tables. When he comes to the till he is carrying two books: *In Praise of Martyrdom* by a highly fashionable Ukrainian writer, and *The Beauty of Cadmium*, the first book—a collection of stories—by a young and hitherto unpublished writer. The bookseller, who recognizes him, asks him why he has chosen these two books. Broto ponders for a moment. The one by the Ukrainian, because everyone is raving about him and he's not read a word by him. The other because he was intrigued by the first sentence—he thought it was beautiful and highly intelligent. He has leafed through the book, and read fragments from the middle and the end. The author employs a rich language but no frills.

He starts reading *In Praise of Martyrdom* at home, but gives up on page thirty. Partly because when he began reading it was late at night, and his eyes closed at page thirty. He sleeps through the night, out for the count. However, when he goes back to it next morning, he reaches page thirty-six and puts it to rest, if not definitively, at least on his shelves, where it may stay for years, never to be opened again. Broto then picks up the other book, the one by the young author—David Guillot—and opens it at the first page. He reads the first story. He finds it more than decent enough. He then reads the second: flawless. Finally he begins the third, also a good one. The fourth doesn't seem quite at the same level, but if it hadn't been for the high quality of the previous stories, it would probably have impressed him favorably. Conversely, the fifth and sixth seem only so-so, and the seventh, predictable. But the eighth tale is very good, the one he likes the most. When he at last comes to the end of the volume, he does so feeling it is an interesting collection, particularly for a first book.

Subsequently, a few months later, when, in the course of an interview, a journalist from the cultural pages of a daily asks him to recommend a book by an author that he's recently read with pleasure, Daniel Broto says: "*The Beauty of Cadmium*, by David Guillot." It is a long interview, over two pages, with a large photo of Broto at his desk, tapping away. The question appears in a box on the second page: "Can you tell us about a recent book that you liked?" Broto replies: "I thought *The Beauty of Cadmium* by David Guillot was very good." He's taken aback. When asked to name a book that he had particularly enjoyed, he gave a title and the author, but hadn't added any special value judgment. However, as he *had* liked the book, he doesn't intend getting worked up over such a small detail.

The day after the publication of the interview, when Broto returns home after his university classes, he finds a message on his answering machine from David Guillot, who—as he says—has read what Broto said about him in the newspaper and simply wants to thank him. It wasn't difficult to deduce how he got hold of his telephone number, because they have it at the publishers where Guillot published his book: from the boss to the head of publicity. He repeats, "Many thanks," several times. And also: "Broto, you can't realize what your words mean to a novice like myself, who has just seen his first book in print. You must know that to be recognized by a prestigious writer like yourself is a present from heaven." He thanks him again, profusely, and leaves a number. He knows, of course, that Broto must have an enormous amount of work and can't afford to waste time on trifles like this—"a young writer who is just beginning, I mean"—but, just on the off chance he might like the idea, he'd be delighted to speak to him, if only on the telephone, especially because Broto is, in Guillot's eyes, a master, the most important living author, the one who guided him through his adolescent scribbling, his literary model even now when he is starting to publish, the example who "if you allow me this little confession, led me to decide to write and become a writer. And I'm really delighted to tell you that, now I have published my first book and . . ." The call breaks off at that point; another call follows on immediately, also from Guillot, who begins by saying: "I see I went on too long. I don't want to be a nuisance. I'll leave you my number just in case you want to call, and that's all; I won't disturb you any further."

Broto jots the number down in the address book he keeps next to the telephone and thinks that maybe he will call him later. Now he sits at his desk, puts some order into his papers, takes his students' texts from his briefcase, puts them in a pile and lights a cigarette. The next day, when he takes his raincoat off the hanger to go to the theatre, he sees the book with the number next to the phone and thinks he'll give him a call tomorrow if he can. But tomorrow comes, and goes, and a new tomorrow comes, and another, and yet another, and there's never a moment to call. One evening when he goes into a book shop, he sees that Guillot's book now sports a wrapper that says: AN EXTRAORDINARY BOOK, DANIEL BROTO. He had never said at any point that it was an extraordinary book. As he remembers it, when asked to recommend a book that he'd recently read and liked, he had replied: "*The Beauty of Cadmium*, by David Guillot." That was it. He had in no way used the words—"I thought it was a very good book"—that the journalist had put into his mouth in the newspaper, nor this other phrase that now presides over the book's cover, in huge letters, even bigger than the title and the author's name: AN EXTRAORDINARY BOOK, DANIEL BROTO. But Broto isn't shocked. It's standard practice for publishers to cut and adapt phrases people say in order to turn them into sound-bites, and he intends to keep his calm.

Then, about a year later, Broto brings out a new book. And one day when he is signing copies in a large department store, he spots Guillot's face at the end of the line of readers who are waiting their turn. He recognizes him from the photo on the jacket flap. He's dressed in black. He is thin and nervous. He looks this way and that, but not at the table where Broto is signing, and the moment their eyes meet, he immediately looks away. When he finally faces Broto, he introduces himself and hands him the book to be signed. He says he telephoned him a year ago, that he left messages on his answering machine, that he was very pleased with the praise he had given him in the newspaper, that this praise meant a lot to him, because, on the one hand, it strengthened him in his determination to write, and, on the other, it had made a decisive impact on the way what he writes is received by the public. For example: he has started writing literary reviews in a newspaper, and he would never have managed that if Broto hadn't spoken so highly about him. Behind Guillot, the line of readers holding books gets longer and longer. "What's more, I must tell you that I am very sorry . . ." says Guillot, and he apologizes for the wrapper they put round the book: that was the publisher's decision, he says, against his wishes, because he didn't want to take advantage of his words, and even less so, in the second edition—which is already out, something quite unusual for a first book—with Broto's phrase printed on the actual cover. "You'll be wishing you'd never read my book, Mr. Broto!" he says, goggling at him. Broto feels embarrassed by all this, and by having to sign his copy of his book now. He tells him not to buy it, that if he leaves his address he will send it with a personal dedication, courtesy of his publishing house. But Guillot says no, no way, he's craving to read his book—"your books are so good, they mean so much for us writers who have just embarked on our apprenticeship!"—and wants him to sign it because that dedication is like a dream come true, as much as being able to talk to him in the flesh. When Broto sees that once he has signed his book, Guillot just stands there holding it and the line gets longer and longer, by way of a goodbye Broto says they could speak on the phone one day and go for a coffee or something of the sort. Really thrilled, Guillot gawps and says of course, whenever he wants, and just in case he has lost the number he left on his answer-machine (in fact he has lost it, or at least hasn't seen it for some time), he jots it down again on a page in the notebook he's carrying in his pocket.

Back home Broto pins Guillot's number on a cork-board next to his desk. Every so often he takes a look at it and thinks he should call him and agree a time to meet. That way, Guillot would be happy and he could forget him, because the situation was beginning to annoy him. He doesn't know why, but he doesn't feel like seeing him one bit. His insistence, his anxious looks, all that sucking-up . . . But time goes by, Broto doesn't ring him and, gradually, the sheet of paper with Guillot's number is buried under other sheets, postcards, bills and calling-cards. Until one day, a good few weeks later, the telephone rings and the answering machine springs into action and Broto can hear Guillot telling him that he knows he must be plowed under but they had said they would call, arrange to meet and talk. Guillot insists he doesn't want to be a nuisance, that he knows Broto must have too much work to waste time on authors who are just starting out, "and there are so many, because more and more are getting into print these days . . ." But if he ever feels like it, he repeats, he would be delighted to have a beer, coffee, or glass of water with him—"I don't know what your poison is, Broto," he says very chummily or, "maybe we can simply speak on the phone," because Guillot would like to run several things past him before taking a decision, particularly because, as far as Guillot is concerned, Broto is a lighthouse, the light of genuine literature in a literary scene that is increasingly mediocre and banal: "And, really, I don't want to be a nuisance. I'll leave you my number in case you've lost the note that I gave you in the department store. How excruciating, right? To have to sign books in department stores, for people who are more struck by the fame of a name than the literary quality of one's work. I'll leave you my number, then. It's . . ."

One day when he is coming out of a radio interview, Broto sees that Guillot is the next on. They shake hands. Guillot says: "Don't say you'll call me, because you know you won't. People sometimes says these things: 'We'll be in touch,' 'I'll give you a call,' but they are often just polite formulas. It doesn't indicate there is a real desire to make it happen. Maybe it will, but circumstances don't help matters, or . . ." But the program producer takes Guillot off into the studio. Broto sighs, pulls up his overcoat lapels, and goes into the street. He does indeed feel vaguely guilty, and that upsets him, because he shouldn't be feeling guilty about anything. But he had certainly told him in the department store that maybe they should be in touch and go for a coffee. But, if you think about it, saying maybe they should be in touch isn't to say that they actually would be in touch. He never said he would give him a call. When Guillot was so annoyingly insistent, Broto said, "maybe we should be in touch." "Maybe" plus a conditional. He didn't commit himself to anything. The only thing he had done—and didn't he regret it now—was to praise this Guillot's first book. He keeps recalling that sentence Guillot uttered in the department store: "You'll be wishing you'd never read my book, Mr. Broto!"

Six months later, Guillot brings out his second book: *The Nature of Zones*. Broto receives it through the post, in one of those envelops padded with little plastic balls and with a dedication on the title page: "I really don't know what to write. This is my second book and I know that, to a very large extent, I owe its appearance to you, because if you hadn't spoken so warmly of the previous one, there would probably have never been other editions and this second book would never have see the light. In any case: you owe me a call. There is no rush. I don't want to take up your time." Broto feels uncomfortable. What does he mean that I owe him a call! I don't owe him anything! He reads the book and he's not sure whether his reaction is triggered by a defense mechanism, but he likes it much less than the first. If he read the first now, would he like it as much as he had before? A few months later, during a talk he is giving at the library in Sitges—in a series—"Conversations with Our Authors"—Broto spots Guillot's accusing eyes in the audience, a Guillot who later addresses him with a smile on his lips. "Didn't you know I lived in Sitges? When I saw you were coming, I thought: I'll go and see what these fellows from the capital have to tell us." At the dinner after the event, Broto sees how Guillot—now transformed into one of the local literary hopefuls—is the focus of attention in a group of two young men and a girl who are laughing and whispering at one end of the table. It is an image he will recall a number of times over the years. When he receives—with no dedication, straight from the publishing house—Guillot's third book, *Apparent Medicine*, and the fourth, *Behind the Colustrum*. And also when Broto publishes a new book and Guillot reviews it in the daily newspaper and questions the exaggerated importance given to this author—In my view, he will write, it quite beggars belief.

The Coming of Spring

A man is in a geriatric residence, visiting. While he walks steadfastly towards his goal—his mother, head down, in a corner of the yard—he notices how almost a dozen old folk are gathered around a small pond by the path that crosses the yard, many in wheel chairs, others with their mouths permanently gaping open, others with both features: in wheel chairs and mouths permanently gaping open. Others merely stare vacantly. When the man walks by he says, "Good morning!" and four or five return his greeting with a sparkle in their eyes: "Good morning!" Good God. Usually only one or two respond.

A man reaches the house where his parents lived until only a few weeks ago. It is the first time he has stepped inside since they left. He opens the door. It is the flat where he passed his childhood years and some of his youth, until one day he left, pleased to be leaving behind forever a world of madness and backstabbing. The man asked for a morning off work (that he will make up for later: one hour extra a day for five days) and that is why, even though it is Wednesday, he can allow himself the luxury of strolling through the bedrooms at this time in the morning—nine o'clock—assessing what has to be done. For the moment: a good sort out. A woman will come and clean, naturally, but first he needs to see the exact state of the place, and throw away the items that have piled up and have no possible future use, and that make the cold walls, painted (white) some fifteen or twenty years ago, even more depressing. There are lots of photos of the man, as a child, on the sideboard and small tables, and, pinned to a board on one of walls, the postcards he sent them from the countries where he lived quite early on. The walls of the bedroom where he used to sleep still display remains of that blue rubbery stuff (it was called Blu Tack, right?) that ironmongers sold for years as the ideal solution for sticking posters on walls without leaving the walls full of pinholes. Until people discovered that while it didn't leave holes, it made an even greater mess by leaving little blue patches that took heaven and earth to remove. And, if you finally did succeed, it would take bits of the last layer of paint with it, and the wall never surrendered its bobbles of gummy blue.

A man reaches a geriatric residence and goes up to room 211. He knows the way by heart: reception, the glass-walled sitting room, the corridor where the same woman always seems to be asleep in the same armchair, the elevator, the bell. His parents are always in their bedroom. It didn't used to be the case. They used to go out on the terrace or into the back patio with the pine trees. When they see him walk in, both sets of eyes light up. "Ooh! Ahh! Look who's here!" It is always the same panorama. His father in bed, breathing with difficulty; he has been hooked up to a respiratory machine for years. He used to get up and sit in a chair, but he doesn't feel like it any more. At the most he gets up to go to the bathroom, and then walks breathlessly back. On the other hand, even though her left leg is so contorted it seems she couldn't ever stand up straight, his mother positions herself behind her walker and, leaning her torso full on it, goes up and down the room: she stumbles against the bed and chair legs, against the cable to the respiratory machine, against the machine itself, against the chest of drawers with the television and the drawers full of little notebooks, against the walls, wardrobe doors, and sides of the bedsheets that belong to the ghosts of all who have died in that same room and who never cease to walk from one corner to another, grumbling. The mother asks the man how work is going, and the man says it is going fine. When he has communicated that scrap of information, the mother nods for a few moments and immediately asks him what kind of work is it exactly. The man tells her, the mother asks him if it is going well. The man says it is, the mother nods and within a few seconds asks after his work again: Exactly what kind of work does he do now? The father takes advantage of a gap in this endless loop to say—yet again, as always—that one little pill would be enough, one of those little pills they give you and that's that, and you can rest forevermore. It's called Anastasia. It is obvious he knows that he means euthanasia, but he loves to say Anastasia, as if he were making fun of old people's uncontrollable tendency to get their words mixed up. The mother suddenly interjects: "He's always harping on with the same story . . ." And she wants to move on from one gripe to another, but it's obvious she can't remember which. This exasperates her, and her rage intensifies. She looks at the father with hate in her eyes and, swinging an arm that she raises (the other clings to the walker), she says: "The fact is he's lost it! Isn't he repeating himself yet again . . . ?" but she can't in the end figure out exactly why she's grousing at him, and this makes her even more indignant, and she repeats the same words as before: "The fact is he's lost it!" She doesn't know why she is grousing at him, it's a grouse like the thousands of grouses she has hurled his way throughout a lifetime. She doesn't know why she's reproaching him, but she maintains the rhetoric, the shouts, and the insults. In fact, hasn't she always been like that? Didn't her grouses always seem demented and crazy? The difference is that, now, she has only the bare bones of her indignation and hatred, and can't put any flesh on them. Her neurons have given up. She used to grouse at him before, and her nimble mind meant she grasped at any idea, or any excuse, to put flesh on the bones, and the situation would end in a god-awful argument, though one basically as senseless as the present spat. Now the reason why so few things she says have any sense is—so they say—senile dementia, but before (ten, twenty, thirty, or forty years ago) they were equally the product of dementia, although it couldn't then be considered to be senile. "The fact is he's lost it!" she's still repeating. The father looks at the man and says: "You see . . . No change there." They've been arguing like that for so long . . . They both look doe-eyed at the son as if he were the one charged with deciding who is the goody and who is the baddy. So the man gets up from the chair, goes over to the window, looks at the people walking down the street, the bus reaching the stop a little further down, and can see, above the porch, Superman taking off his hero's uniform—tight-fitting top, trunks, and leotards—and putting on shirt, pants, jacket, spectacles in order to turn back into Clark Kent.

A man is pacing around the flat where his parents had once lived. It is a very silent flat. It helps being so high: an attic above ten flats: the noise from the cars doesn't reach that far. When he looks through the large window on the terrace he can see the new tram pass by, between two distant buildings. He gathers together the paintings—that had always hung in the same place; never a single change—the wedding photos and diplomas and puts them all in the same bedroom. He will decide what to do with them another day. Then he goes over to the dining-room table, oval-shaped and made of very shiny wood, that a furniture-maker made when his mother—who adored the furniture in one of the houses she cleaned at one period in her life—wanted the exact same dining room they had in that house. The exact same style, with bookcases, a table, chairs and a red and black sofa, but smaller because obviously their flat was a small one. This table has always wobbled, and still wobbles, because the metal legs are only screwed in, and any knock makes them shift a few millimeters, enough for them not to be entirely stable. As a child, that shifting used to stress him out, and when he was older, whenever he visited his parents, he would always, on the sly, pull the legs out so the table didn't wobble so much. He doesn't pull them out now. Now he takes the table, turns it over, and unscrews the screws from the legs with his fingers—they are so loose they soon ease out of the holes—and leaves it in the hall, to take down later on. He also deposits there the broken flowerpots from the terrace.

One bitterly cold February morning, a man reaches a geriatric residence, goes straight to his parents' bedroom and, as is almost always the case, finds his father in bed and his mother sitting on a chair with her arms draped over the walker. Great joy. They exchange the usual initial words ("How is everything? The family OK . . . ?"), but shortly—after a series of glances exchanged between father and mother—it is clear they want to tell him something special ("Well, boy, we'll cut to the quick . . .") and the quick is that they have decided to commit suicide. The man listens to them in silence.

"We've been thinking about it seriously. All this," the father makes a big sweep with his hand, as if taking in the whole room, "all this is pointless. It is exhausting. It is lasting too long. You know, boy, it's not easy to depart this world."

"Well, I don't know," says the mother, "you do get yourself into a twist like a Venetian blind. Go on, get it off your chest, or if not, we'll be here for a couple of hours, and the lad's got work to do. He can't stand here waiting all this time . . ."

"OK, I'll tell you straight. First we thought we'd throw ourselves out the window," says the father, "but I think that's too melodramatic, and we don't like making a spectacle."

The man looks at the window, the trees a few yards away, the hill you can see, and the city beyond that. He tries to imagine them falling on the canopy over the door and the canvas where it says RESIDENCE FOR THE ELDERLY. The mother shakes her head and grunts: "Where would you get the strength to pull yourself up to the window? Where would you get the strength? I've told you time and again, he comes out with crazy ideas . . ."

"Don't take any notice of her," the father goes on. "This is serious talk. Obviously, the window isn't on. Impossible. Just imagine everybody looking. That would be most unpleasant. It would have to be something more discreet, and that's why we thought about cutting our veins. But there's a problem there too."

"And that is that they would find the blood," says the mother.

"Let me explain," says the father. "The problem is that, if we cut our veins in the shower, which is the logical thing to do so as not to spatter everything, then the blood would go down the drain and show up in the outlets of the showers in the other rooms, so when people saw blood coming through the holes in their shower trays, they'd soon want to know where that blood was coming from and would find us before we were dead."

"I've heard on the TV," says the mother, "that the human body has ten pints of blood. Ten pints. So, as I've got two buckets for washing clothes, because everyone here is filthy and they don't wash anything properly, and I wash my own bras, so . . . Because all these old people, the thousand morons living in this home, couldn't care less, and can no longer tell the difference between what's clean and what isn't . . ."

"The buckets," said the father.

"Well, as I've got two buckets and each holds ten pints, when we cut our veins we will fill the two buckets and then no one will see any blood coming up in any shower tray."

The three of them look at each other in silence for a while. That is to say: the son looks at the parents and the parents look at him. There's a brass band playing in the street. A military parade? A street party? Finally the man says: "So that's how you've decided to commit suicide, is it? Cutting your veins."

"Yes," says the father, "but you've got to be brave and know how to cut them properly . . . And what if it's not as easy as it seems? Young people lose a lot of blood because they have blood to donate or to sell, but us old folk . . . I reckon that us old folk have so little blood that there must be very little difference between having the little blood we have and losing most of it. I'm not sure that old folk can lose most of their blood, or, and think carefully about what I'm saying, or can go on living even when they do. Frankly, it's one big mess, my son."

"The best option," says the mother, "would be not to eat."

"That's the best solution," the father agrees for once.

"That would be very easy for me," says the mother, "given I eat so little, but your father, who eats and eats and can never get enough . . . Do you think he could stand not eating?"

The man decides to tell them that a woman he knew, who was also in a geriatric residence, committed suicide that way: by stopping eating. They seem hardly interested in her, either as a model for what they are proposing to do or as proof that it is a practical suicide.

"So," says the father, "maybe this is what we will do."

Then the mother tells him that some of the girls who come to the residence—those who clean the rooms—steal items of clothing: blouses, knickers . . . The man listens in silence, he's been here before, and then looks at his watch and leaves.

In the evening, the man calls the residence to find out how they have spent the rest of the day. The father tells him he managed to stand not eating lunch, and that he didn't eat dinner either. "You just see how I don't eat, my son." The man thinks that it will be different tomorrow, and that when it's time for breakfast, he won't keep it up. But when he calls the following night, the father declares that he hasn't eaten breakfast, lunch, or supper that day either. The man then talks to his mother, to see if it is true, but his mother doesn't remember seeing her husband eat breakfast, lunch, or supper. When he says goodbye and hangs up, he calls back and talks to reception. They say it's true they've both not eaten anything the whole day. He tells them about the conversation on the previous day and they take note.

So he calls again the next day. Mid-morning. The father answers: "I tell you, son, I really had made my mind up. The day before yesterday, after you left, I didn't eat anything else in the whole day—anything at all!—and I didn't eat anything yesterday either. But tonight, my boy . . . It must have been twelve o'clock: I was starving to death, I got up and ate a banana."

In a flat where nobody has lived for years, a man opens the drawers where his parents—who were the people who used to live there— kept the plates and glasses of the dinner service that they bought for the day he got married, when he took his first communion. But he never did marry and the crockery is still there, untouched; they never even used a glass. Now it is covered in dust. The dust floats through the room like glitter in a children's story. He can see three damaged glasses in the rows of glasses for water, wine, and liqueurs. Two have cracked bases, so cracked they can hardly stand up; the other has a chipped edge. The man can't fathom why they kept them if they were broken, and neither can he understand why they kept two empty olive oil bottles among the glasses: one glass and one plastic, and still labeled. He also finds candle ends that were maybe white at some stage, but are now a dark yellow turning to brown, and some of these ends are an inch or so long and the wicks are burnt. He finds plastic bags in the drawers of the sideboard. Not five or six. Dozens and dozens of plastic bags stuffed inside other plastic bags. He goes on opening cupboards and finds bags everywhere. There must be thousands of brand new supermarket bags that his mother grabbed in handfuls on every visit she made to the supermarket and then stored—why? Out of foresight? Out of fear of shortages in the future?

He doesn't dare throw anything away. He feels rather like an intruder in a well-preserved sanctuary, and partly fears that one day his parents will recover, come home, find it is all changed, and will scream at him like when he was a kid and didn't do exactly what they wanted. He is still afraid they will scold him! But they never will come back, although he doesn't realize this now. For a moment he contemplates putting the oval-shape table together again and back where it once stood, and returning the broken flowerpots to the terrace. Their world was built on the basis of broken items they never threw out, *just in case*. The refrigerator is also old, rusty, encrusted with dirt, and he doesn't dare touch it because—whenever he paid them a visit—they told him never to throw it out, that it was a very good refrigerator, that they don't make them like that any more. The boiler for the central heating is also a very good one, and of the kind they don't make any more. "It's a Junkers!" they'd tell him. As if there weren't Junkers any more or a thousand other top-dollar heating systems. Neither should he ever throw out the washing machine, even though it's been so rusted up—for more than ten years—that it seemed impossible clothes could emerge from it clean; even though it was a leg short and they put telephone books underneath so it didn't tip over.

There are suitcases on top of the cupboards. The suitcase father took with him when he emigrated to Germany in the mid-Sixties, to a city near Bielefeld by the name of Wiedenbrück. He lasted precisely a fortnight before coming back with his tail between his legs. And which was the suitcase mother took to Geneva, when she went into service in the household of the Turkish ambassador, on that other journey—the first having failed—that was to save them all from poverty and transform them into first-class Europeans? There was also the trunk she brought with her many, many years before from Andalusia, its inside lined with pages from newspapers that were so old they were already antique when the man, as a child, opened it, read them, and was fascinated by news that spoke of other eras and of a world war—they still didn't know how it was going to end. When he opens it he spots, at the bottom of the huge trunk, a tiny box with the pastry tube they filled with cream or melted chocolate when they wanted to write good wishes on their cakes, like "Many Happy Returns" or "Happy Birthday." It is made of cardboard and decorated with a colored drawing of a happy family—mother, girl and boy; the father isn't there—decorating a cake with a tube just like that one. Next to the box is his father's free public transport pass, and half of his mother's false teeth. It is the bottom half and is missing four teeth.

A man is watching how his father finds it hard to breathe even though he is always connected to the respiratory machine, and wonders if it is selfish to feel totally fed up and not see any end to this string of years—seven by now—that this very slow death agony has lasted and that is sucking his life away with feelings of sorrow and impotence. At this point in time, his only aim in the world is to stay alive until they die, never to fail them, to be at the end of their beds whenever he is needed, whether it's his or hers. One day, several weeks ago, he had lunch with an old girlfriend whose father had recently died, and she told him that, on the last night, when it was increasingly obvious her father was in his death agony, she took his hand and repeated silently to herself: "Die, die, die, die . . ."

A man is pondering the fact that, until now, it was always father or mother—one or the other—who had to be hospitalized in an emergency. It was generally his father, and this was understandable, because he was the one, from as long as he could remember, who had had the poorest health. Already when the man was a child, when he played at the foot of his parents' bed with wooden building blocks— painted in primary colors—he knew that his father was repeatedly ill. Indeed, he was so often in bed that the man (then a child) thought that it was normal for his father to be at home almost every day with one illness or another. "I won't last long . . ." his father would say then. And also: "For the short time left to me in this world . . ." But after a few days, he would go back to work, whether he liked it or not; though not for long, that's for sure, because immediately—after a maximum of a few weeks—he would be back on sick leave. Having sick leave for father was the proof that he knew how to get the most out of life. He uttered those same words—sick leave—with the same respect that other people utter the name of the king, the author of the best history book ever written or the scientist who has discovered the most sought after vaccine. "I've been given sick leave," he would say proudly. It was obvious and understandable that father didn't like working, because the work he did didn't interest him in the slightest—who could be interested in wasting life inside a factory, day in, day out—and he would sing the praises of those (and there were quite a number like him) who managed to avoid work as much as they could, and he spoke of them as examples to be followed, and even boasted about working as little as possible. To succeed in running one lot of sick leave into another was his main aim in life. And he so persevered in this vein that with the passage of time he succeeded, not so much in getting occasional sick leave, as living in a kind of perpetual sick leave that was occasionally interrupted by the odd day in work. Until finally, one glorious day when the sun cracked stones and the angels in the heavens praised the goodness of God, he received the big news: "Signed off because of chronic illness." His father would have shouted, "Wicked!" if the victory cry at the time had been that, as it was later. But it wasn't at the time, and that is why the man simply remembers the blissful smile on the smooth features of his father, who must have been a little over forty. It meant his total victory in life. He stopped working forever and started receiving a minimum state pension, but the joy at not having to step foot in the factory ever again was more than enough compensation for any financial shortfall they would all now have to endure, though, since they had never ever been exactly flush, they didn't suffer too much. The son never worked out which of the many illnesses his father had suffered simultaneously over the years had granted him the grace of a partial invalidity and had, finally, blessed him with permanent sick leave. From that moment on father became set in a strict routine: he was always at home, but not now in bed, as before, when leave was merely temporary, and he thought he needed to pretend and at least wear pajamas in case an inspector appeared. (He didn't remember any inspector ever visiting their house, but the mere word conjured up respect and fear). Once he had entered the Paradise of Permanent Sick Leave, he had no need to pretend, and every morning he would go for a walk in the neighborhood or take the tram or metro and go to his childhood neighborhood and see friends who still hung out in the bars where, as a young man, he had lived the happiest days of his life. When he didn't go out he would sit on the sofa and listen to the radio, and it soon became obvious that it was necessary to buy a television to keep him entertained in all those dead and empty hours he now had in the day. Thus, within weeks, the first television set arrived in the house, a huge, mass-produced box, that would accompany them in their married life—in black and white—until long after the son left home and for decades watched his father's illnesses from afar—heart, liver, kidneys, and lungs reduced to a rag by sixty years of cigarettes and dust from the items of clothing he breathed in the factory, perpetually suffering that illness they call chronic lung obstruction and that has tied him to a respiratory machine for the past six years. Besides, naturally, the cancer of the bladder that, for fifteen years, has involved visits to the city's most prestigious oncology center and which he would survive thanks to a then-new method that—in his case, as he had never had tuberculosis—consisted in injecting him with that virus, provoking a reaction in his body that eliminated the cancer, as well as the tuberculosis. This whole sorry record, complete with bloody sputum, continuous tightness in the chest, and perpetual, sharp back pains, meant that over the years he is the one that generally needs the most attention, and that most often, when the situation gets out of hand, has to be hospitalized, always in an ambulance that crosses the northern area of the city, via a route that takes in packed streets and avenues running alongside parks that the man and his father have never seen before, but that now—as admissions to the hospital have become regular events—have finally become familiar to both of them.

But this year it is the wife who has speeded up the process of degeneration. She had always been the strong partner, the one who worked nonstop, who slept four hours, who, when she finished her job on the production line, came home and saw to everything, who cooked, who swept, who mopped, who never let anyone help her, who, to save money, made their shirts, pants, coats, skirts, sheets on the sewing-machine . . . That house had never bought anything in a clothes shop, not even a handkerchief, because she even made their handkerchiefs with the sewing machine that had been such a good investment. She was also the one who put up shelves on the wall, if they were needed, who repaired them with mastic, who varnished them, who climbed the ladder to paint ceilings and walls, who gave the rails on the balcony a coat of red-lead, who every so often switched the furniture around because she got bored seeing it always in the same place. She was the one who built the standard lamps from a steel tube, a dumb-bell disk, an electrical cable, a connection, and a bulb-holder. She was the one who prepared the coquilles Saint-Jacques and took them to the bakery, five streets down the hill and was the one who never stopped for a minute, so she didn't have to wonder what she ought to be doing in that minute when she had stopped. She was never still for a moment, never stopped doing something for a second, had always been the healthy partner, refusing to go to the doctor's "because doctors are all morons and know nothing about anything" and yet now, since last spring, she is the one who is always falling: she falls down in the bathroom after getting up from the toilet, she falls in the bathroom when she is washing her face—she loses her balance and tries to grab the sink, but it doesn't work because her arms are now too weak to bear her weight—she falls in the bathroom when she is trying to hang up the bras she has washed, falls on the floor when she leaves the bathroom, falls on the floor when she tries to sit on a chair, and falls on the floor when she's getting up from the chair. She falls on the floor because one of her legs is completely twisted by the arthritis she refused to have treatment for—"because doctors are a load of morons"—when the first symptoms of the illness appeared. She falls on the floor when she walks to the window and also when going over to the entertainment center where they keep the television and two huge drawers full of hundreds of little mass-produced sandwiches, all wrapped in cellophane and past their eat-by date, that she doesn't eat so as to be able to keep them in those drawers for months and years. She never eats them, but that makes no difference. She keeps them with the same passion with which, before going to live in the residence, she stuffed her cupboards with plastic bags, thousands upon thousands of supermarket plastic bags, that she grabbed by the handful whenever she went to buy anything—three potatoes, an onion, fifty grams of ham—and just as she now hoards boxes of aspirins and adhesive for her false teeth on a shelf. She also falls when she is in bed: she rolls over and, unaware she is on the edge, tumbles to the floor. She has occasionally split her head open, and since last spring, when the process of degeneration began to accelerate, to the end of summer she began to be unable, sometimes, to hold things in her hands. She would pick up a cup and the cup fell on the floor. She would pick up her glasses and the glasses would fall on the floor before she had had time to put them on. So it was soon plain enough that a worrying change had taken place, all the more so when the moment came when she no longer recognized what was being said to her nor could manage to articulate a single word—she began one and with great difficulty managed a syllable and by the second had forgotten what she wanted to say—so she had to be hospitalized, and that was a great upheaval for her husband, so much so that, at the time his wife was being admitted, whenever he spoke to his son on the phone, he used to remind him that he too was very sick, that he found it increasingly difficult to breathe and the sputum was black, rather than green, with the added factor that his back pain was more acute than ever. "I know that mother is ill, poor dear, but so am I . . ." Poor father too, who had always been center-stage when it came to illness and now feels momentarily displaced by his wife and this high blood pressure that needs constant care, so that when the son makes his escape really late one evening from the hospital where his mother is and visits his father for a while so he doesn't feel abandoned, father tells him he has a temperature, and when the son puts his hand to his forehead and tells him he doesn't, his father says he is sure he does, and when the son puts the thermometer there and they see it registering 98.3 degrees, the father, tears welling, swears the thermometer isn't working properly. The son understands his father's disarray: he has always been sicker than anyone, and now, all of a sudden, the fact his wife is worse pushes him out of the limelight. Consequently, when his wife improves slightly and returns to the residency, the father is pleased, but, afterwards, whenever they admit her again, he repeats (ever more threateningly) that he is also very sick and that if he bears up and says nothing it is because he can see that his son, poor boy, is having a rough time, what with work and them, and he is afraid he'll be ill too: a heart attack or something similar, God forbid. And one day, while the man is accompanying his mother to the hospital in an ambulance, he gets a call on his cell phone from the residency. They have just ordered another ambulance for his father, who has had an anxiety attack and is finding it difficult to breathe even with his extra oxygen supply. He is still in the emergency room when his father's ambulance arrives, so that he divides his time between one bed (situated in a room with nine other people) and the other (at the end of a corridor, next to the bathroom). When, after several hours of waiting, they put one on one floor, and the next day, the other on another, the man thinks it would have been even worse if they had admitted them into different hospitals. As it is, he simply spends the day going from the coronary unit to the pulmonology floor. One evening when he is particularly tired, he sits in a chair opposite his father, who is devouring his dinner with an enthusiasm he never loses. When he sees him looking so despondent, the father half wipes his lips on a serviette, lifts a finger, and says out of a half-filled mouth: "You look sickly, boy . . . Look after yourself, my lad. Look after yourself, make sure you look after yourself, because if anything happens to you, what will become of us?"

One night a man dreams he must bury the dead, and with the greatest respect, so nobody can say: "They weren't buried with proper respect." And it is not because others think he must bury them with respect, but because after entire lives that have veered from being half-happy to wretched, what else could he do but give them a dignified farewell and try to erase the less pleasant moments from his memory? That is why he is keen to find a place where they can rest forever. But which? That spot over there by the wall of their house isn't the place, because it is far too dismal—they may have lived a sad life, but they don't deserve that much gloom. Conversely, the closed in space is fine, because it has a yew tree and they were fond of trees. No sooner said than done. He cleans the area up, removes the stones and weeds, and flattens out the ground. After that, he takes his van and drives in search of the most decent coffins: neither too ostentatious nor too mean. He salvages the fork and spade from the cellar, where they have languished for decades (ever since they were no longer capable of using them) together with axes and hoes. And stops at this point. He can do no more. He knows he must bury the dead, he is fully conscious of that, although there are people who think he isn't and sometimes they tell him so in the street, without realizing that however much they remind him and put pressure on him, he can't bury them, because they are still alive.

Stunned by the painful old age of his father, who has been asking to die for years, a man ruminates day and night, turns it over in his mind time and again, but however many turns he gives it, he never manages to imagine the great paradox: that, when his father finally dies, he will feel really upset. Because finally they will have succeeded, finally father will have died as he had been demanding to, but at that moment, what his son would most like to have done in this world would be to hug him and say: "That's it, it's all over, life has ended, exactly as you wanted." In fact, he will hug him and tell him that, but his father can't share his happiness precisely because he is dead, and the fact that it is impossible he can ever know that he is dead, having so craved to die, will break his son's heart.

One day, a man decides that he must kill his parents, who are old and on life's final slope. It is what they have wanted for years; sometimes they even tell him how they dream of doing it, but clearly they don't dare. The man often contemplates his father dozing and sees himself grabbing a pillow and covering his face. It would be so simple—maybe one or two minutes?—and his father would then be granted the peace he so craves. And wouldn't death be the best present a son can give a mother, who has calculated how many buckets she will need to collect all the blood from her body. He looks around the room; the three of them are alone. It would be so easy to splash gasoline everywhere and set fire to it. And all these other old folk in the other bedrooms wouldn't be able to make a run for it either. Everything would burn, not a single wall would be left standing, and for many relatives there would be tears of woe, but also of relief. However, whenever he imagines it, he sees his father and his mother appear, turning the wheels of their chairs with their hands, in the midst of the debris and smoke, among the corpses of the other residents: "Son, you don't know how frightened we were!" And then, at the burial of the dead—all the other residents would have died, apart from them—he would see his parents cry out of a mixture of sorrow and liberation. And the next time he goes to see his parents, in another residence (because they would take their time to re-build the other), the mother returned to her endless loop, the father talked about euthanasia, suicide, and the pills he kept on his bedside table during those last years he lived at home, for when he couldn't stand it any more.

His mother is in her chair, asleep. His father is in bed, on his side, breathing as breathlessly as usual. The man looks out of the window. If it were spring he would see trees with branches full of leaves but it is winter still, and he only sees bare branches and, in the distance, the smog over the city.

2

"Mum," said little Serge when he woke up, "a man came and wee-weed in my bed last night."
—Roland Topor
Alibi d'enfant

Next Month's Blood

In the reign of good King Herod there came to the sparse village of Nazareth a woman by the name of Mary, married to a good-natured carpenter, Joseph.

One splendid spring morning, the archangel Gabriel visited the woman and told her: "God has blessed you with his grace, Mary; the Lord is with you."

She found the words of the wingèd one bewildering. Why did he greet her with so much ceremony? The archangel spoke: "God has decided that you will have a son: you will call him Jesus."

Mary struggled to understand what he meant, so the archangel repeated his words to her: "Don't be afraid, Mary, God has granted you the grace of a son; you will call him Jesus."

But Mary refused, point-blank. "What do you mean, no?" asked the archangel, at a loss. Mary didn't backtrack: "No way. I don't agree. I won't have this son."

Thirty Lines

The writer begins typing cautiously. He has a short story to write. Recently, people have been talking about the virtues of short fiction, but, if he were to be frank, he would confess that he detests stories in general and short ones in particular. Nonetheless, to keep in the swim, he has been forced to join the band of fakers pretending to be passionate about brevity. Consequently, he is terrified by how lightly his fingers run along the keys, one word flowing after another, and another, and then another, finally shaping into a line behind which another—and another!—are already forming, yet still he can't focus on a theme, because he is trained for long distances: he sometimes needs a hundred pages before he gets a glimpse of what he is going to write about, and at others not even two hundred suffice. He has never once worried about length. The longer, the better: blessed be each new line, because, one after the other, they reveal the size and the splendor of his work, and consequently, even though two or fifty lines add nothing to the story he is telling, at the end of the day, he never axes a single one. Conversely, to write this story he would almost need to take a tape measure and measure it. It is absurd. It's like asking a marathon runner to run a hundred meters with dignity. In a story, each new line isn't one more line, but one less, and in this case, specifically, one line less up to thirty, because the rubric is: "Between one and thirty lines," in the voice of the old fellow who called him from a newspaper's Sunday supplement to ask him for a story. The writer reluctantly lifts his fingers off the keys and counts the lines he has written so far: twenty-three. He has only seven to go to reach thirty. But, after he has registered that insight—plus this one—even less remain: six. Good God! He is incapable of having a thought and not typing it, so each new one eats up a new line and that means by line twenty-six he realizes he is only four lines from the end and hasn't succeeded in focusing the story, perhaps because—and he has suspected this for a long time—he has nothing to say, and although he usually manages to hide the fact by dint of writing pages and yet more pages, this damned short story makes it quite clear, and explains why he sighs when he reaches line twenty-nine and, with a not entirely justified feeling of failure, puts the final full-stop on the thirtieth.

A Cut

Toni dashes into the classroom with a look of terror in his eyes and a gash in his neck. It is a deep, broad cut, spurting blood that is bright crimson rather than red. One would say, on the evidence of a glance, without a proper investigation, that, now that the flesh has opened up, the gash—that in principle should be no more than a millimeter wide—is two to three centimeters across. We might estimate its length at twenty to twenty-five centimeters, given that it starts under his left ear, goes down his neck, and ends level with his chest, slightly to the right of his sternum.

"They attacked me with a broken bottle."

Blood is seeping down his neck, staining the white shirt of his uniform. His jacket collar is equally soaked in blood.

"Come on, boy. Is this any way to walk into the classroom, Toni?"

"Sir, Ferran and Roger got hold of a broken bottle next to the vending machine, stuck it into me, and . . ."

"How does one enter the classroom, Toni? Is this how one comes into a class? Does one enter any old way? Does one enter without saying 'Good morning'? Is this what we have taught you at school?"

"Good morning," says Toni, putting his right hand over the gash to try to staunch the flow of blood.

"Generally speaking, habits have been degenerating, and you are not to blame, I know. We are also to blame, in institutions that are unable to offer an education that shapes character with a proper sense of discipline and duty. But society is also to blame, and all the many parents who demand that school provides the authority they are incapable of wielding. You, Toni, are but a sample, a grain of sand from the interminable beach of universal disorder. Where is the discipline of yesteryear? Where are the sacrifice and effort? Where are the basics of education and civility we have inculcated into you day after day, from the moment you entered this institution? I know that many other educational institutions practice a much laxer form of education, and that, as it is impossible to totally isolate each individual, and being aware of the tendency of the youth to mingle and fraternize, I know, for all these reasons, that, however much our institution strives to educate you in exemplary fashion, if we are the only ones inculcating any norms, you have too great an opportunity to be polluted by the lax mores of others."

"Sir, I'm soaked in blood."

"So I see. And I can also see the dreadful mess you are leaving on the parquet. Not to mention your shirt and your jacket. You know by now that I like your uniforms to always be spotless. But we will leave that for tomorrow. Now go to reception and ask Mr. Manolo for a mop and a bucket of water and try not to splatter blood all down the corridor, as you will have to clean that too."

One Night

Plum in the center of the room, the prince can see the body of the girl, who is sleeping on a litter of oak branches and wrapped round in flowers of every color. He quickly dismounts and kneels by her side. He takes her hand. It is cold. And her white face, too, like a dead girl's. Not to mention her thin, purple lips. Conscious of his role in the story, the prince kisses her lovingly. He knows this is the kiss that must bring her back to life, the kiss the princess has been waiting for forever, since the witch's curse put her to sleep. The prince leans his head backwards so he can gaze at her when she lifts her eyelids and opens those large, almond eyes.

But the girl is still asleep. Perhaps, thinks the prince, he kissed her too lightly. He stoops down again and kisses her a second time, this time a touch more vigorously. However, the princess doesn't wake up. The prince persists. He squeezes the girl's cheeks with his index fingers and his thumbs so her mouth opens slightly, to make the kiss more intense. Then he puts his tongue inside, curls it around hers, takes it out, nibbles her upper lip, and immediately afterwards her lower lip. He kisses her ardently, as he has rarely kissed anyone before. These kisses arouse the prince. He feels something swelling in his crotch that soon hurts because of the tight tutu he is wearing. But then he restrains himself because he reckons that, when the girl wakes up, he will be able to unleash the passion that is coursing through him. He is certain that the girl will wake up feeling equally passionate.

Nonetheless, however much he kisses her, the princess doesn't wake up. The prince stops for a moment, caresses her cheeks, and immediately starts to kiss her again: he kisses her repeatedly, ever more energetically. What kind of prince in blue is he, if his kisses aren't able to wake up the sleeping maiden? Princes in blue always boast about waking up princesses with a single but irresistible kiss. He feels useless, and is thankful that at least no one else is in the room watching him.

Things should be going differently. He should kiss her and she should wake up. He has been at it for a quarter of an hour and both their lips have swollen because the kisses were so passionate. He now unbuttons the girl's blouse and gazes at her breasts: round, pert, and perfect. He looks in awe at her nipples that are large and pinky brown. When he inspects them closely, they suggest the porous quality of a lunar landscape. He wets them with his tongue, clamps them between his lips and sucks hard: first one and then the other. Maybe his kisses don't wake her, but this should do the trick. Just in case the nipple licking has made no impact, he brings his lips back to hers and kisses her ardently. He puts his hand under her skirt, strokes her thighs, and reaches the vertex they form with the pubis. Finally he lifts her skirt completely up and gazes at her legs that are pale, tensed, soft, and simply splendid. He gradually lifts her body with one hand and takes her panties off with the other. He kneels down in front of her, separates her legs and the lips he finds there. He brings his mouth down on her, licks her, flickers his tongue in there, runs it along each fold in the most intimate kiss—he believes, in his innocence—that a prince has ever given a princess. This is the definitive kiss, he thinks, the kiss that awakens sleeping princesses. He lingers there awhile, and the more he lingers, the more he is aroused, until, unable to contain himself any longer and ruminating that perhaps the business of the kiss is only a metaphor for a more radical form of contact, he pulls down his tutu and inserts himself between the girl's legs. He moves in and out, first slowly and then ever more forcefully, until each thrust shakes her whole body. But even so she doesn't wake up. Disappointed, the prince stops, withdraws, and rests his head on the girl's bosom. He is tired and makes a space on the litter next to her, and he gazes at her. She is so beautiful that he soon feels passion returning, overwhelming him again. The girl still doesn't wake up. He spends the whole night in this state, and returns to the breech ever more convinced that sooner or later she will wake up, but he is the one who falls asleep at the break of dawn, exhausted, embracing her body. A few minutes later the girl stirs, looks at him for a second—he is so handsome—shakes his arm off, and gets up, feeling out of sorts. What is this sleep she is awaking from? How long ago did she close her eyes? She struggles to remember anything, and gradually walks off. The prince is sleeping deeply, unaware that nobody will ever come to wake him up.

Another Night

S ometimes, when the man goes to the cinema he finds himself watching films in which occasional sequences contain characters who go to bed and read for a while before they go to sleep. The light shines from their bedside table, and to emphasize the act of reading, they often put their glasses on, but now and then read without them. Some are all alone in bed and some are accompanied. When they are accompanied, the other person is also usually reading. Generally they read books, but sometimes magazines or newspapers and, in the occasional film in which the character has to demonstrate that he is obsessed with his work, even dossiers and reports. But—as noted—they are generally reading books and after a while they switch off the light and fall peacefully asleep. Sometimes sleep hits them so suddenly they don't have time to switch off the light and close their eyes with their books open on their chests and their glasses dangling, so that one day the temples get twisted. The man is fascinated by the sleep-inducing nature of books and knows that it is no product of the fantasy of film-makers because, for example, when his wife has been reading for a while, she closes her eyes and falls into a deep sleep. On the other hand, it never happens to him. If he gets into bed at night, even though he is feeling rather sleepy and is yawning, and opens the book on his bedside table, he unerringly feels his neurons perk up and, passionately drawn in by the story-line, he reads page after page for hours and sometimes notices that his wife has switched off her bedside light and is turning restlessly in bed because his light annoys her and, as he is loathe to annoy her, he gets up and goes off to read on the sofa. Because of his good intentions to sleep and wake up rested in the morning, the worst thing is that, when he does finally close his book and put out the light, the fiction keeps going round in his head: the characters unravel their idiosyncrasies and the plot, and buzz with a thousand endless possibilities. Then the insomniac phase kicks in and he doesn't get to sleep until dawn, and sometimes not even then.

Initially, the man thinks this is happening because, after so many years of reading, he has nurtured a certain talent for separating the wheat from the chaff and the books he reads are frankly very good. He rarely gets it wrong. He tried to solve his problem by looking for mediocre efforts. He would go to the bookshop and ask for poorly structured novels, far-fetched stories, collections of doggerel and tales that couldn't hook anyone, that were so boring they sent any reader to sleep after a few minutes. But not even these fictions could send him to sleep, because his neurons perked up just the same, not because he was enjoying the party—as with good books—but because he was imagining solutions to the various crazy loose ends. And so the crack of dawn would find him still turning over how to resolve contrived situations, unlikely loves, and shoehorned murders. Until he reached the conclusion that perhaps the problem was fiction. If he chose biographies, for example, he would quickly fall asleep because there was no creative tension. But he soon found that wasn't true either and that there is often the same creative tension between a real life and a fictional life. So then he opted for magazines. He bought women's magazines, magazines about decorating, motorcycles and knitting—subjects that had hardly ever interested him. But the fact was that, as soon as he began to read, his interest was aroused and he was soon passionate about vintage Harleys, Charlotte of Monaco, and Shetland wool. Not even do-it-yourself magazines put him to sleep, because he imagines how, with four planks and a few screws, he could erect the shelves they sorely need, the ones his wife has been nagging him about for some time, a unit that is so specific they will never find one ready-made anywhere. And it is even worse when he is tossing and turning in bed because he can't get to sleep, and his wife (whom he has never told about his insomnia, so as not to worry her) turns towards him, seeks out his body, and within seconds they start to fuck. This is the worst because, no sooner have they finished than the man is about to pleasantly drop off when, between flickering eyelashes, he sees she is wide awake, looking at him and grumbling: "You're not falling asleep already?"

Beyond the Sore

A **party.** Music, drinks, food, various euphoriants. The house has a garden with statues. Far off, in the distance, one can see the city. The woman is saying to the man she met a while ago: "This view makes me think of *Beyond the Sore*." The man hesitates for a moment. He knows she is talking about a fashionable new book but *he* hasn't read it. To buy some time, he asks her as if he's unsure: "*Beyond the Sore*?" She says: "Yes, *Beyond the Sore*, by Anthony Spiniello." He says: "Oh, yes, of course."

It will look dreadful if the man confesses he hasn't read it. Though that is the truth. Even though she has said the landscape reminds her of the book, it is quite possible she hasn't read it either, so—whatever he says—he's not taking that much of a risk. But if he dares to say anything it is because, at the very least, he is up to speed with the four comments one must make about the book. He is thinking that it isn't a crime not to read books. Countless people don't. But he is next to the woman he has been hovering around ever since he joined the party and, now that she deigns to talk to him, he is at a loss about what to reply. He could say: "No, I've not read it. The fact is that recently I've only been re-reading the classics." He knows that for years when asked in interviews about the current books he was reading, Terenci Moix would always respond that he was re-reading the classics, period. In theory, it is a strategy one can only use if one really has read the classics. Because the interviewer could then ask you which classic you are re-reading and, if he knows it, he would catch you out.

But that is only in theory, because in practice the ruse can be used without running into problems. Nowadays, the likelihood one will run into somebody who has read a particular classic is minuscule. Nonetheless, just in case, he ponders over what else he could say. He could say: "The fact is I read so many books that I never remember the plots. I know I liked it." That is *not* a lame response. Even Montaigne was often unable to remember what he was reading. He smiled nervously. He could make four vague statements and not enter into detail. If he had taken more notice of the cover the day he saw it at the bookstore, at least he could discuss the quality of the design and wonder what the hell it had to do with the contents. If he had read one of the reviews the book has received . . . One day, when he was in the elevator at the firm where he works, he overheard two women talking about *Beyond the Sore*. If he had focused on what they were saying, he could repeat it now. If they said it was a marvelous book, he could say that it is marvelous. If they said it was weak, he could say it is weak. This is the heart of the matter: never introduce a discordant note, be gray among the gray, never stand out among those who never stand out. But time goes by and he has to say something; he finally decides: "Well, you know, I think that its greatest merit is the way it conceals a truly awesome narrative beneath mind-bending simplicity." Her eyes gaze at him, sparkling with champagne. She asks: "Doesn't it vaguely remind you of *Perfume* by Patrick Süskind?" He hasn't read *Perfume* either (he's not even seen the film), but he doesn't intend wasting any more time. He smiles and relates: "Don't mention perfumes to me.

I was in a restaurant for lunch, about to take a sip of cream of carrot soup with *foie*, when a man drenched in eau de cologne walked in; he quite killed off the aromas from the whole menu." She laughed theatrically. In fact, she didn't think the anecdote particularly amusing but, as she likes the man, she leans her head backwards and he takes the opportunity to place a kiss on her cheek.

Many Happy Returns

One day, an ophthalmologist friend of mine decides to tidy the section of the conjugal wardrobe that is his. He is mindful of the fact that he has five or six jerseys, on the top shelf, the corner with the items he never wears. Most have v-necks and all are in shades that go from yellow to ocher. What are they doing there?

They have been accumulating dust for years. How many exactly? Some may have been there for six or seven. Others possibly ten even. He once put one on, took a look in the mirror, and wore it for a while. But took it off before leaving the house. He has never liked v-necks or pale shades for jerseys. And although he finds yellow the most acceptable of all pale colors, he does not like it. He likes dark colors. Especially black and dark gray.

But the woman he lives with—his wife—simply adores pale colored jerseys, particularly in shades that go from yellow to ocher, and especially if they are v-necked. She has never understood how her husband—my ophthalmologist friend—isn't mad about these pale shades and this kind of neck. Subsequently, convinced that perseverance is the mother of enlightenment, every birthday, saint's day or celebration she gives him a v-necked, yellow to ocher shade of jersey, although it is quite true that on a particular, very distant occasion she did give him a gray one. Pearl gray, naturally, because she likes pale shades.

My friend's wife is sure that, by dint of persisting, he will one day realize he has cultivated a blind-spot all these years, refusing to admire the beauty of pale shades and v-necked jerseys. That is why he decided to ignore the fact that the jerseys she gives him keep piling up on his section of the top shelf of their wardrobe, one or two more every year. It is a good idea to put the new ones on top, because, that way, the layer of dust has always to start afresh on the front of the new arrival.

And given that—if she always gave him jerseys—they wouldn't fit on the shelf (even though it is a big shelf), what she now does is give him records occasionally. And, as she wants to give him the best, she buys him her favorites: Paganini, Mendelssohn, Arriaga, Glinka . . . The height of Romantic music, which is what drives her crazy. But Romantic music doesn't appeal to my friend the ophthalmologist in the slightest. Just as he doesn't like the Thomas Mann novels she also gives him. According to her, Thomas Mann is the summit of universal literature and she is sure that, if my friend would only get to the end of one, he would immediately see her point.

But she never relents. If we take into account that he is the person she wants to make happy, she could give him—exactly—what he likes: dark gray or black jerseys, music by Béla Fleck or Pascal Comelade, books by Ben Marcus or Neil LaBute. But that would be to surrender, and she is sure that, if she doesn't relent, some day her husband will be the one to surrender. He will listen to one of the records she gives him—all the way through: won't take it off after a couple of minutes—or will wear one of those yellow to ocher jerseys and go into the street and see that they do quite suit him. That will be the start: from then on, with even more perseverance on her part, he will gradually begin to resemble—day after day, little by little—the man she wished he was.

Things Aren't What They Used to Be

Marta has always felt nostalgic about her childhood, that childhood when, though they had a television, her father, mother and nine siblings sat around the table at suppertime and nobody dreamed of asking for the television to be switched on. Because at suppertime they recounted what they had done during the day.

"Today, we studied primates at school," Marta would say.

"Oh, really," her father would respond, sounding interested.

"Would you like some more lettuce?" her mother would ask.

When Marta had a son, primates were no longer studied: they were a worksheet. They did worksheets on primates, quartz, stalactites, and the vegetable world.

"Today we did a worksheet on holy trees," her son told her.

Marta would have liked her son to grow up in that same atmosphere of healthy fraternal cheerfulness. But, to start with, Marta had had only one son, and with only one son, there can be no fraternal life, be it healthy or otherwise. Besides, television had ceased to be outlawed and was gaining ground by the day.

She tried to fight against it for a while but soon threw in the towel, and at meals, the whole family—she, her husband, and their kid—allowed the television to be head of the table. Then Marta would criticize it: "It isn't good for us to let television rule our lives. We don't communicate anymore. Can we have so little to say to one other?"

Her husband thought differently: "But isn't it time for the news?"

It was always the same: as soon as they were sitting around the table, her husband would switch on the television. And their child immediately learned the lesson from his father and—if at the beginning he also argued: "It's time for the news"—he soon had no need to hide behind the alibi of the news and, rather than the news, it began to be Formula One races, supposedly acerbic cartoons, or programs with celebrities who sat around, taking turns insulting each other. *Communication* between family members had begun to go downhill and would never ever climb back up. As soon as they finished eating, all three leapt on to the three-piece suite and there they didn't communicate due to competitions, dancing, and trite chat shows. She would have preferred a game of dominos, which allows for minimal conversation, a gentle exchange of ideas, but she had accepted a long time ago that it was a lost battle and she couldn't go against the flow of history.

But now, for quite a few months—a year, maybe two, or more—Marta had begun to wax nostalgic even for those times, when she, her husband, and their kid spent the night in front of the television. Because—she could never have imagined this—they now communicate even less. From the moment the first computer entered the house, everything changed. First there was only one computer, but now there are two. Her husband uses one and her son the other. She doesn't want a computer. She receives her e-mails at work and sends them from there, and if she ever does need to send something urgently from home, she uses her son's or her husband's. But now what happens is that, as soon as they have finished supper, her son collects up the dishes and takes them to the kitchen, her husband fills the dishwasher and switches it on, and they both immediately closet themselves in, one in his office, the other in his bedroom, and she is left alone on the sofa, in front of the television, feeling nostalgic for the days when, at least, that screen meant they spent a while together.

The Fullness of Summer

They are all related. They meet three or four times a year and this is their summer reunion. They usually arrange to have lunch, and today is no exception. They come from different cities and rendezvous two hours before, in one of their homes, a vast flat with sea views. There are a lot of them. A genuinely large family from the days when families were really large and not like now, when large is three children. Amid loud shrieks of joy—"Hellooo!"—they kiss each other and, as there are dozens of them, the rounds of kisses mean the kissing phase is so prolonged that, when they finish, it is almost time to jump into their cars and head for the restaurant where they have a reservation. So, displaying the same joy with which they greeted each other on arrival, they now rush out shouting, "Follow me!" and, "See you at the restaurant!"

When their cars drive up, it is as if they're reuniting after centuries apart, and they thus repeat their greetings—"Hellooo!"—and the kisses. Given that, as mentioned earlier, there are dozens of them, it takes a long time to make the rounds. But the restaurant is no stranger to meals of this nature and, consequently, the waiters are in no hurry to start serving, because, however time much they took, they would find everyone still in the pecking phase. The fact is that when they finish kissing they still have a good half hour to wait for the *tapas* first course, and they use that time to take photos. Photos of everybody together in front of the restaurant entrance. Photos of genuinely married couples. Photos of individuals. Photos of the children by themselves. Photos of the children with the older folk. Everybody smiling, even the two dominant males of the species who are competing to show off their expertise with digital cameras. A rivalry that extends even to the moment when the waiters finally start to serve the meal and they walk along the extremely long table, taking fresh photos of all the people they had snapped outside and who now compete to see who can smile the most spectacularly, and the longest, so much so that some individuals sustain their smiles through the hours that slowly elapse between desserts, coffees, cigarettes, cigars, and postprandial chat, until finally it is goodbye time again, with fresh rounds of kisses, and the last photo sessions before they climb into their cars to drive—in one caravan—to the flat where they had met before lunch and where, as they arrive, they greet one another—"Hellooo!"—and kiss anew, before going in for an immediate viewing, on the television screen, of every single photo the dominant males of the species have taken before, during, and after the meal. "Look, there's little Laura!" says Silvia, as if it were a miracle that little Laura is there, snapped while eating her veal and champignons. It is less than three hours since little Laura was eating her veal and champignons (that at this very moment must be a magnificent alimentary bolus coasting through her intestine) and they can already see her on screen! This excites them to no end. And provokes reflections like: "People can say what they like, but before we had digital photos you had to take the film to be developed and you couldn't see the photos of the meal on the same afternoon!" Just the kind of thing to keep them in a frothy state of bliss that lasts until it is time for each and every one to go home when there is another round of kisses and—as there are dozens of them and the necessary turn-taking so everybody can kiss everybody is never-ending—it is very late by the time they finish. "But as it is summer, it's still light!" says little Laura, radiating happiness, while her husband starts up the car and she smiles and waves and photographs the people smiling and waving and photographing her from all the other cars.

The Boy and the Woman

The boy is walking down the street with a rucksack full of fliers hanging over his shoulder on a single strap and a roll of sticky tape in one hand. He sports a trimmed beard and a green parka. He deftly cuts four pieces of tape, takes a flier from his rucksack and sticks it on a wall. He has been doing this for the last half hour. He sticks the fliers next to shops and door-entrances. But also on streetlights, mailboxes and even on trees. On the fliers he's posting up today, above two cell phone numbers it reads: "Flat for sale c/ València, 3 rms, 1 dble. Kitchen+ gallery. 16sq.mtr terrace. Very light. Old-style. 237,399 euros." Every day the flats on offer on the fliers are different. More expensive or cheaper. More or less rooms. No terrace or new build. Lots of potential or fantastic views. Totally refurbished or luminous and in need of renovation. Ready to move into or ideally situated. Stone-tiled floors or very well serviced. Ideal for couples or no agencies please. Brand new, newly built, fully renovated, or two bathrooms. Or three bath. Very sunny or excellently situated. Near the metro. Ideal investment. In perfect condition. Kitchen-diner. Flawless. Parquet floors. Better than new. Elevator. Two elevators. The estate agents give him different fliers everyday. It took him ages on the first few days. He needed fifteen seconds to take out the piece of paper, cut the bits of tape, attach them to each corner, and stick the flier to the wall. Now five seconds are more than enough.

The woman has been trailing him for some time. It is very easy to follow his tracks; you only have to go from one flier to the next. The woman watches the boy from a distance. He is in front of a building, putting a flier in place. When she finally draws level with him, he is already sticking another a little further on. The woman stops in front of the façade, carefully pulls down the flier the boy has just stuck there, and throws it into a plastic bag she is holding. The boy stops, about to attach the last of the four pieces of tape he uses for each flier. They look at each other for a moment. The boy finally attaches the piece of tape and walks off. The woman goes straight to this other flier, carefully detaches it, screws it into a ball, and puts it into the plastic bag. As he walks along, the boy turns for a second to take a glance at her. Then, he starts to put a flier in place on the adjacent building. The woman stands next to him and waits for him to finish. When he has finished, she pulls down the flier, screws it into a ball and stuffs it in her bag.

"Hey, what do you think you're doing?" asks the boy.

"I'll pull down as many fliers as you can put up," she answers.

"You know, this is how I earn my living. I have all the right in the world to stick fliers on walls!"

"I don't think you have any right to stick fliers on walls. In fact, I don't think you have any right at all. But now isn't the time to argue about that. And, in any case, I have all the right in the world to keep pulling them down, and that's what I intend to do."

The boy walks away as far as a lamppost, deftly cuts four pieces of tape and sticks up a flier. When he finishes, the woman is already next to him, and she pulls the flier down, crumples it into a ball and stuffs it in her plastic bag. The boy accelerates to the mailbox on the corner of the street, puts another flier in place, and the woman takes it down immediately when she gets there, while he rushes towards a tree where he attaches a flier the woman runs at and swiftly detaches, because, now, as he sees the woman is tearing down every flier he puts up, the boy attaches them less firmly.

After several hours the boy stops. His rucksack is empty. The woman stops as well and takes advantage of the pause to empty the balls of paper into a bin. She has already emptied the bag twice. The boy has posted all the fliers the estate agency gave him, but as the woman kept tearing them down, there are none to be seen anywhere. They eye one another suspiciously, quite some distance apart, and say goodbye with a "See you tomorrow."

The Fork

This takes place on a sunny Sunday in the month of April, in a restaurant in a village situated in the foothills of a mountain that still has a snowy peak. At lunchtime, with most of the tables still empty, two couples arrive, nearer sixty than fifty. One of the men walks into the dining room avidly reading a sporting daily. It is obvious they often come to the restaurant, because they greet the *maîtresse* very informally, with a kiss on the cheek, and talk about how long it has been since they last saw each other. "It was before Easter Week!" one of the women says, pretending to be surprised. Then they talk about their children. Apparently they are all well. When that exchange is at an end, the owner (smiling as always) points them to the table she has reserved for them. It is an oblong one, to one side of the dining room. One of the women chooses one of the chairs next to the wall and the other, the one opposite. The husbands will also face each other but on the passage side.

Then, while they are still standing up and taking their coats off, one of the women quite by chance bumps a fork, hers, and it drops silently on the floor—even though there aren't many people in the dining room, the background music drowns out every other sound and, additionally, voices from the kitchen are audible. The other three don't notice that the fork dropped on the floor. The other couple is now facing the wall, and gazing at a painting where you can see a cypress-lined path on a yellowish morning, and the husband of the woman who caused the fork to drop on the floor is still absorbed in his sporting daily.

The woman moves swiftly to retrieve the fork. However, rather than leaving it to one side of the table for the waiter to change for a clean one, she takes her husband's fork and places it where hers was, and the one she has just retrieved she puts on the left of his plate, the place once occupied by the fork she has appropriated. Then she sits down. Her husband subsequently sits down, hints that he has finished reading his paper, and folds it.

I observe them, quite fascinated. Why didn't she ask the waiter to change her fork? If she doesn't mind the fact it dropped on the floor, if she thinks it is fine to use it even though it got dirty, why didn't she put it back where it was, next to her plate? Some people aren't at all bothered if a piece of cutlery or item of food falls on the floor. An imaginary Five Second Law operates among young Americans, according to which, if something falls on the floor (a roll, a piece of cutlery . . .), nothing untoward will happen if you retrieve it within five seconds, since, they argue, the dirt, microbes, or whatever need more time to infect the item that has been dropped. But the lady clearly can't believe in this law, because after retrieving the fork she didn't consider it clean enough for her to use. Although it was clean enough for him. Is he less persnickety? Do years of cohabitation rot even stones? Is it a sample from the many other small acts of revenge she practices? Does she also spit into her husband's breakfast cup of coffee whenever he yawns?

I then review the few busy tables in the dining room. No diner has noticed what she did. The owner hasn't either, or the waiter, a very efficient young man who right now is taking them a full breadbasket, some olives, and the menus with the dishes for the day. The other couple finally stops looking at the painting and sits down. They pick up the menus, open them and start to read.

Shiatsu

It's a great bar, a favorite in the neighborhood, with maybe the best ham in Barcelona, and hocks—done in the oven with onion, tomato, pepper, white wine, and cognac—of the highest quality. There are four tables in total. Two are square, and a man is breakfasting at each—one is bald and the other has a mustache—and two are rectangular, and exactly double the size of the square ones. A man is sitting at one of these tables and he has long white hair and is wearing a blue tracksuit. The other rectangular table is free and that is where the four people now entering the bar head, laughing and joking and brandishing folders. They sit down, take off their coats and scarves and hang them on the stand near this table that was free till now, and also on a chair by the table for one that's next door. Before leaving his anorak there, one of the newcomers asks the man with the mustache who is sitting there: "Is it free?" When the man says it is, he takes the chair, pulls it over to his table and puts his anorak there.

Before even a single minute has passed, three more people come in, also carrying folders—that are from an institute for traditional Chinese medicine that's immediately opposite—and they loudly hail the four who came in before them. When they reach the table they look both ways, making it clear to everyone that they are wondering where to sit. They don't do this at all unconsciously, because this is their way of disturbing the customers who are eating breakfast and reading their newspapers at the other tables. As a result of this gesture, they immediately make the man with long white hair and a blue tracksuit who is breakfasting at the big table feel uneasy, and he rushes to finish his coffee and get up. He is still in the process of standing up when one of the newcomers accosts him and asks, looking anxious: "Are you leaving?" The man answers: "Yes, of course." Two of the newcomers quickly grab the table and, when their hands are underneath, about to lift it up, they turn to the bar manageress and ask: "Can we put the tables together?" She says they can, and thus they take good hold of the table and shift it next to the one they have already occupied, but as there's not enough space to fit the new large table between that one and the square one next door—where the bald man is having breakfast—they push the small table to one side, and their efforts push the small table and bald man a yard towards the bar, lodging them against a stool. As a result, once the new table is slotted in, the newcomers can finally sit down—all seven of them—around the two tables they have joined together, something they celebrate with great hilarity and the odd shout. However, this maneuver means the door to the ladies' bathroom is blocked and the hooks, where customers have hung their coats, are now out of reach. This circumstance allows the newcomers to lean their heads back on a comfy cushion of clothing. When the waiter comes they order: a tea, a *ristretto* with skimmed milk, a Coca-cola and a croissant, another—decaf—*ristretto*, a single *espresso*, and a latte in a glass.

It soon becomes clear, nonetheless, that even with the rearranged tables there is still not enough room, because the door to the bar opens again and five more people walk in—all carrying folders from the institute for traditional Chinese medicine—who laugh and shout as they head over to the people at the two joined tables. When they see there is only room for one of them, they look around the bar. There are hardly any options. One of the student newcomers takes the initiative, approaches the bald man's table and asks him if he can take the chair where nobody is sitting. The man has his coat there, and it is now impossible to hang it on the coat hooks: he can't reach them because the remainder of the students and the rearranged tables block the way. So the man takes his coat, drapes it over his legs, and says: "Take the chair." The young man takes it and places it by the table they now occupy, but the students keep staring at him. They do so in the belief that the fact there are a lot of them gives them superior rights. It is a stare that says: "There are a lot of us. How come you don't immediately lift your butt off that chair and clear off, given there's only one of you, and leave that place for us, because there is a gang of us and numerical superiority grants us that right?" That their insistent stare has the desired effect soon becomes obvious when the bald man gets up and goes to the bar. He is still paying when the students from the institute for traditional Chinese medicine take possession of his table, push it next to the two others they already occupy and sit down. But it is apparent that even with this domino trio of tables they still don't have enough space: there are twelve of them and only eleven can fit around the three tables because one side is up against the wall. That's why in a determined yet discreet process of expansion the twelfth in the group chooses, out of all the chairs at the three combined tables to share, the one nearest to the man with the mustache who is locked against one of the stools at the bar and who is thus pressed even harder against the stool. Accidental knocks and big flourishes of arms up the ante. "Oh, so sorry," they say the first time he is hit, but the second and third times, they say nothing, and when he gives them a scathing glance, they all look up in unison to challenge him, and although in principle the man tells himself he is not prepared to give in, that he doesn't see why he should, that just because they are in the majority they don't have any right to chase him from his table, and he doesn't understand why the manageress, who has a notice over the coffee machine that says RIGHT OF ADMISSION RESERVED, doesn't exercise *her* right and at the very least ask them to behave politely. But soon the accidental knocks become deliberate and increasingly outrageous, and they so pile on the pressure—now he hears them pushing to shouts of "Come on, altogether: wow, wow, wow!"—he gets up and pays. As he is going into the street to the gleeful victory cries of the throng inside, he has to move aside yet again because three more individuals sweep in with their folders from the institute for traditional Chinese medicine, masters now of the whole of that bar they have finally succeeded in making their very own.

Quim Monzó was born in Barcelona in 1952. He has been awarded the National Award, the City of Barcelona Award, the Prudenci Bertrana Award, the El Temps Award, the Lletra d'Or Prize for the best book of the year, and the Catalan Writers' Award; he has been awarded *Serra d'Or* magazine's prestigious Critics' Award four times. He has also translated numerous authors into Catalan, including Truman Capote, J.D. Salinger, and Ernest Hemingway. His novel, *Gasoline*, and short story collection, *Guadalajara*, are also available from Open Letter Books.

Peter Bush is an award-winning translator who lives in Barcelona. Recent translations are Juan Goytisolo's *Níjar Country*, Teresa Solana's *A Shortcut to Paradise*, and Alain Badiou's *In Praise of Love*. Current projects include Najat el Hachmi's *The Body Hunter* and Josep Pla's *The Gray Notebook*.

Open Letter—the University of Rochester's nonprofit, literary translation press—is one of only a handful of publishing houses dedicated to increasing access to world literature for English readers. Publishing ten titles in translation each year, Open Letter searches for works that are extraordinary and influential, works that we hope will become the classics of tomorrow.

Making world literature available in English is crucial to opening our cultural borders, and its availability plays a vital role in maintaining a healthy and vibrant book culture. Open Letter strives to cultivate an audience for these works by helping readers discover imaginative, stunning works of fiction and poetry, and by creating a constellation of international writing that is engaging, stimulating, and enduring.

Current and forthcoming titles from Open Letter include works from Bulgaria, Germany, Iceland, Italy, Russia, South Africa, and many other countries.

www.openletterbooks.org